CHAO
PB

SO-AIN-035

Because Cuba is You
Ramón Chao

Translated by Ann Wright

Middletown Public Library
West Main Rd.
Middletown, RI 02842

route

12/14/2013

First published by Route in 2013
PO Box 167, Pontefract, WF8 4WW
info@route-online.com
www.route-online.com

ISBN: 978-1901927-50-4

Ramón Chao asserts his moral right to be
identified as the author of this book

Original edition:
Porque Cuba Eres Tú, 2005

English language translation © Ann Wright

Design:
GOLDEN
www.wearegolden.co.uk

Printed and bound by CPI Group (UK) Ltd, Croydon, CR0 4YY

A catalogue for this book is available from the British Library

All rights reserved
No reproduction of this text without written permission

Route is supported by Arts Council England

To my descendents in chronological order:
Manu, Antoine, Jaime, Kirà, Merlin…

In Cuba
Beautiful island of burning sun
Under her azure sky
Adorable brunette, of all the flowers
The queen is
You.

And contemplating you
My lyre sighs
Blessing you, peerless beauty… ay!
Because Cuba is
You.

Fernán Sánchez/ E. Sánchez Fuentes, 'Tú'

Chapter One

ONE DAY, ONE OF THE MANY on which my grandmother awoke consumed by nostalgia, she began to tell me her nightmare of the previous night as if she were living it.

I was in a field looking up at the sky, scenes from my childhood floating by in the clouds. My footsteps left their imprint on the path; in some places a pair of footprints, in others, two pairs. The first matched my feet; the others, over them, seemed like copies, so alike were they. As I came to the end of the path, I looked back and saw that at the most distressing moments of my life, there was only one pair of footprints. I was truly sad and implored whoever accompanied me:

'I would like you beside me always, yet in the most difficult parts of the journey, only my footsteps are there. I cannot imagine why you leave me alone when I need you most.'

I heard a disembodied voice reverberating in the air.

'You will come to understand that I never abandon you in your hours of suffering. When there is only one pair of footprints, it is because I am holding you in my arms.'

She picks up a calendar, runs her fingers over the velvety surface, and stops on the 27th July. The other dates appear untouched, unused; they had never marked a precise time, the limits of each day and each night.

I have been vegetating here a long time. Five, or perhaps six, ten years. I live with my solitude; I talk to it, to my distress, to my conscience. I can put the world in my room, asleep in the sun that filters through the magnolias.

When I came back from Cuba, my son Xosé allotted me this room, which for guests bears the number seven. There are always rooms free. What angels would come blowing around these godforsaken parts? The hotel slowly empties and the new travellers do not make their mark.

Since that time, so many years ago (it seems to have passed without intervals, days and nights), my grandmother has hardly left her room. She has turned it into her study and bedroom, with the River Magdalena beyond, distant yet visible. Even while the well was dynamited below her window, she sat impassively, her face to the light, like one more piece of furniture, a household relic waiting for who knows what; not death I hope.

Past passions had to recoil when they beat on her windows and dissolved on some obscure interior plane. A procession of bodies crossed paths and faded into memories that I must now revive.

I wonder why, in my circumstances, I need to circumscribe my life by words; perhaps I imagine the writing of them will make sense of all that has happened to me.

Perhaps now she can gather together the impressions dispersed throughout her lifetime. Ideas come tumbling in. First... no, there is no first or second, or even time, or else the time span lacks any distinct boundaries. Despite everything, she is able to face herself, look herself in her light-filled yet imperceptibly dimming eyes.

I don't know why I find it so hard to tell what I know I must without digressing. It is the first time I have considered recording my painful memories: because before, merely contemplating them liberated me. Now I need to bring order to the confusion: put words on paper, lots of words, to see if I can create the tiniest jot of coherence.

She no longer knew what there was to remember; it was no use forcing her memory, as if outside pressure could pursue each picture and capture it. Caressing the pages of the calendar in the mornings until she lost heart did not help, nor did repeating under her breath, like a litany, the day, month, year and name of the saint written in small letters below the date.

SHE WOULD BE IN HER SIXTIES. At this stage of her life, she was called Señora. Previously she had been Dolores, Lola, Lolita – in descending order – and Loliña as a child. She had been born in the Galician village of Lanzós, one of those godforsaken places scattered along the mountainsides where goats would climb, if there were any. It is separated from the river by three barriers: a large piece of stony ground burnt by the sun, some dusty barren fields, and a cow track of mossy stones.

The village consists of fifty hovels strung out along an acacia-lined road. The flora is not very varied; apart from wheat and rye, gorse grows on the hillside, and round the houses you find nettles. The fauna comprises three cocks for fifty hens, a mare, a dozen cows, twenty pigs, and a donkey. In addition, each house has several dogs, the beds are home to gangs of bugs, and the air is thick with an infinite number of flies. As for the human population, although you get to know them all almost at once, it is hard to put a number on them.

When the gods were handing out gifts to mortals, each land was given virtues and defects that were transmitted to those born there. Apparently sexual potency was given to the Japanese, love of poetry to the Walloons, confidence to the Italians, good orderly behaviour to the people of Aragón, a sweet nature to the Basques, and so on and so forth until it came to the Galicians, who got only wisdom and fantasy.

It is true that very strange things happen here. There is a mystery in our land beyond the mist, beyond the sea, the rain and the woods. The land has its own destiny just like humans and even animals. I always told myself that we who are born in this land at the end of the world have a guiding star, or a cross to bear, because there is always one that comes a cropper.

The weather in Lanzós is like a fizzy drink, freezing in winter and an inferno in the summer, almost biblical: a plague, the twelve plagues of Egypt. When the river level drops, a steamy bed of stones appears in the sun, flies stick to the necks of cows and donkeys, to wine and to soup. Those who venture out into the street, mostly dogs and children, are quickly enveloped in a cloud of dust.

The population is divided into three categories: the upper class consists of the doctor and the schoolteacher; the middle class of the priest, his housekeeper and a corporal in the civil guard; and the lower class is the fifty or sixty people who make up the rest. This tripartite division is based on social considerations but there are others too: between military and civilian, industry and agriculture, and so on, always in pairs, because Lanzós is a microcosm in which there are no customs, only life.

Villagers get their supplies at Miragaya's store. He is a short, robust fellow, something of a philosopher and saint. In his tavern, he sells wine and food. When there is a good harvest, the wine is bitter; when there is not, it is mixed. Women gossip in the doorways, men inside; kids and dogs everywhere. Miragaya spends long hours meditating. Apart from putting up with four regular drunks and waiting for potential ones, he spends his day lounging about, always with an eye for the main chance. He wears black for his wife, dead some two years back. People say, or it may be apocryphal, that when Mariquiña, as she was called, was facing the grim reaper, she asked her husband several times if he had been unfaithful to her. The poor woman was so insistent − 'go on, tell me so I can die in peace' − that Miragaya leaned towards her, kissed her between her eyes and said very lovingly:

'And what if you don't die?'

THE DESCRIPTION OF MY GRANDMOTHER by those who knew her match the memories I have of her melancholy expression, still abundant breasts, and hair between blond and brown depending on the angle.

Hair colours change with the land. In the Cuban sun, we brunettes go blonder, or more auburn, but here, with so much rain, our brown hair is darker. With the slightest ray of sunshine, our skins go an olive brown colour, as if we're painted with black smoke, a custom very frowned upon in Labana outside Corpus Christi or Christmas. On those days, black people were allowed to dress up as little angels or carnival princesses.

In grandmother's room is a photo of herself aged twelve, leaning against the back of a sofa (part of the photographer's set, no doubt) with a carnation in her hand. She is dressed simply, not that far

10

removed from a uniform, her shirt sleeves down to her wrists. The silk ribbon around her neck does nothing to lighten the overall modesty of her clothes. The only note of coquetry is her hair, covered by a scarf decorated with Moorish patterns that falls to her waist; a refined little girl, in contrast to her rustic family. She does not look pretty, but her expression is unsettling. Her face has a look of sad anxiety, as if a question is about to spring from her lips: Why? What world is this? What have I done wrong?

Her mother, versed in astrological calculations, saw that the little girl's horoscope was lucky. Although she would face hardships and tribulations before she reached fifteen, if she passed this test with flying colours, there would be joy and possessions for her on this earth.

THE PLACE KNOWN AS LANZÓS is far from the capital. It is identical to all the other villages in the region: two rows of hovels for human beings, shared with a few animals, so poor, so low, that the hens wander around on the roof tiles.

Sad and small, I imagined other places would be bigger, maybe with more people, but one village was much like the next: we went from Mass to the vegetable plots, from the fields to sleep. But once a year at our festival, the sky was lit by fireworks.

A fiesta was not a fiesta without pyrotechnics. By the magnitude of the explosions, even from far away, you could guess the wealth or penury of the village, the number of people attending, the route of the procession and the amount of food families were stuffing down their guests' throats.

There was no cinema, radio or anything: village people just let their imaginations rip and their tongues wag. Galicians love stories, whatever comes into their heads, invented or exaggerated, any old story will do, just as long as we don't have to spend all night staring at the fire.

After Mass, meetings were held in the church hall for local people, easy fodder for the merchants of blessed illusions. Bagpipes and tambourines would follow. In time, orchestras with big bass drums and cymbals came all the way from Irimia, the county town. The atrium ran alongside a cemetery with its gothic niches for the dead, visible and spectral; fertility and death rolled into one as couples amused themselves in nocturnal excesses.

THE SCHOOL OPENED in 1876. It was paid for by the Masonic Club of La Habana. It seemed only natural that when emigrants returned – now Cubans par excellence – they should build cultural centres in towns and villages that were so neglected by the state.

It stood on the Monteto Redondo; large with a well-tiled sloping roof, a terrace looking south and a balcony looking towards the Samarugo pathway.

The emigrants' benevolence did not stop at erecting new buildings or restoring existing ones; they always went further. Their constructions brought together all the hygienic, pedagogic and architectural advances recommended in the doctrines of *compagnon* Jules Ferry.

When Graciano came back from Cuba to inaugurate it, he was recovering from hemiplegia. Although the gods had smiled on his adventures in the cigar business, he lived and dressed more poorly than a beggar, and only ever wore rags. He covered his head with a hat of fallen bird wings that looked like a parasol, and by way of a suit wore a wicker mat round his body, although what most heralded his tightfistedness were his shoes, nailed together by tacks and mended in the most elementary fashion. In a nutshell, this man, whom fate had showered with honours and riches, led a life that the very disciples of Crates of Thebes would envy. However, so that everyone would believe he lived in luxury and ostentation, he had collected funds in Cuba so he could be magnanimous with his village.

'The first absolutely necessity, if Galicia is to emerge from the dire situation in which it finds itself,' said Graciano grandiloquently as he handed over the keys of the school, 'if we don't want our

12

children to disappear off to foreign climes, if they are to be prepared for the future of glory and wellbeing to which their abilities summon them, is to raise the level of culture of our country, and provide an education concomitant with the greatest achievements of the 19th century, and the march of modern times.'

There was something sad in Graciano's eyes, I think, and if he smiled, which he did not usually do, it was as if he were asking you to pity him and smile back.

The final act was to appoint a school concierge. Because what makes institutions is not the members, nor the President, nor the board of directors, nor the rule book, it is the concierge. An institution exists if it has a caretaker, if possible with braided uniform and epaulettes. With the appointment of Miragaya, the Lanzós school was declared open for business. And lo and behold, the tavern keeper was converted by decree from a complete ignoramus who could barely read and write, into a illustrious man, expert in the ways of the world; a leading light, versed in all manner of matters; to the extent that the fame of his wisdom was trumpeted through the villages, and everyone took him for a mine of information.

Chapter Two

LIKE A GOODLY NUMBER OF EMIGRANTS, Graciano had lived in Cuba since he was a boy. Starting work in the cigar workshops at an early age, he progressed without major difficulty up the rungs of the ladder until he became an expert cigar twister. In 1864, he acquired a few fields from his employer and from there went on to own thousands of hectares of tobacco plantation employing hundreds of *guajiros,* which is what freed negroes came to be called.

It was customary in the cigar factories to distract the workers and improve their productivity by reading *Romeo and Juliet, The Count of Monte Cristo,* or other melodramas, which gave their names to makes of cigar. In Graciano's factory they read short stories in Galician, and poems by Eduardo Pondal, who sometimes recited them himself since he was a friend of Graciano and lived in La Habana: '*Que din os rumorosos/dos prados verdescentes.*' Eyes popping out of their sockets, the *bembón* negroes tried to understand that archaic language.

The Ten Years' War ruined many landowners, in the manner in which rich people are ruined. Incursions by the *mambís* laid waste the plains of Rio Seco, in San Juan y Martínez, where nine hundred families worked.

The major part of the calamity, however, passed Graciano by. He retired to La Habana where, driven by his love of opera, he sought a job as an usher in the Tacón theatre. He saved enough money to return to Galicia and exhibit the riches he had acquired overseas. In former times, returning emigrants, known as *indianos,* came back with fob watches which chimed like Big Ben; in the 1950s and 1960s it was flash cars (Pontiac, Cadillac, Studebaker...), when

I was a boy in the 1940s they would bring back three diamonds, possibly from Cuervo y Hermanos: one in a tie pin, another on a little finger, and another on a watch chain that spanned their girths like a military sash over their raw linen waistcoats. The biggest show-offs would swing the watch arrogantly, and pawn it on their return.

'DISEMBARKING AT VIGO I was reminded of Santiago de Cuba with its steep hilly streets, and where one of the squares is also called Colón. I believe the terraced inlets round the shores, like an amphitheatre, can hold all the fleets of the world. In the middle of the bay is an island, and others equally sheer and rocky guard its entrance. Those who come home ruined from the Americas are wont to say that is where their treasure trunk fell into the sea. The peaks surrounding the city are covered in pine groves. And Vigo produces delicious chocolates. I bought a box for the family.'

Worn out by the voyage, yearning for Galicia, at his age Graciano already felt like a stone dropping in a curve, a few inches from the earth.

'Once I was off the ship I felt better, doubtless because of the ozone. It smelt like Cuba after a cyclone, when the wind changes direction. Purifying rain, an extravagance of water without direction, like me, oozing endlessly out of who knows what hole in the sky. The cold gripped my lungs as if I were breathing shards of ice. And thorns grew inside me like a vine feeding on my own breath.'

ONE NIGHT, luck – or the Devil who doesn't always sleep – would have it that Loliña and Graciano would return from a country fair together.

'I have nothing to give you, child. At the very most, I'll live another ten years. You'll be twenty-five and you don't want to carry a corpse with you all your life.'

'A scrap of life for the doors you open for me.'

In the darkness they sought each other's hands: one soft, diminutive; the other large, rough.

'Señor Graciano, how come you were born in this country and not in Cuba, which must be more beautiful?'

'I left here as a boy. Someone born in a village seeks the horizon until he reaches it. Imagine what it is like to live in mud and snow with an empty stomach. A poor man's life is a bottomless pit; he even has to leave his land, though he still carries it inside him. Poverty is the worst kind of misfortune. Yet the land where one is born is merciful; and no one is cast out. How many Galicians have returned to their village after sixty years and stayed to end their days? Because you don't forget your family even if letters never pass between you.'

'So where do you like living best, here or there?'

'For Galicians, Cuba is a paradise. But not one of them, as far as I know, forgets Galicia, even if he never sees it again. He lives in one country with his thoughts and tongue in another, because language is ensconced in the brain from the moment you hear it from your forefathers. Most of the time, when I am in Cuba and am talking to myself, I feel things more deeply if I say them in Galician. Stories my grandparents told still ring in my ears, songs and all. They didn't want me to hear because I would be afraid in the night. But I hid behind a chair and learned all about the werewolf who sucked the blood of damsels; the fox who entered the village and carried off a little angel in his fangs; and especially the story of the moon growing cold and turning us into statues like Sodom and Gomorrah, which is why, apparently, they went rigid staring into the void, their eyes white with terror.'

'How frightening! And where is that town Gomorrea? Near Lanzós?'

'I'll explain it to you when you're grown.'

'Many come home to die, Señor Graciano. And I will too if one day I leave this hole. But Galicia is my land; here I was born and grew to be a girl, here I want to die, and if I am to be

16

buried somewhere, I'd like it to be in these parts. And you, Señor Graciano, did you reappear so I could meet you?'

'To deserve you if I can, and try to offer you a new life. Call me Graciano, Loliña, I'm old enough to be your father, or even your grandfather.'

'My father lies in the graveyard. I don't want that pain again. What do I care about the difference in age, if we share the same dreams? You have had so much more life, experience, travels. I didn't know my grandparents, not on my father's side nor my mother's.'

'And how long will you be in mourning for your father?'

'We grieve for our fathers for five years. And rejoice for another five.'

The image of my father magnifies when I look back over a distance of half a century. I would have been seven. I remember him bent double, riding his horse, from village to village, trading calves or pregnant cows. He was what they call a merchant, arranging cattle deals for the Lugo Estanqueiro. He also leased land and planted maize. Sometimes, before getting off his horse, because I was the youngest he would sweep me up in his arms. Sitting me on the animal's neck, he took me for a ride at full pelt while my sister grumbled that it was her he should have taken.

IN THE MORNINGS, the fields, soft with dew, awaken with different shades of green, marked differences of tone between the darker humid shadow, and the sunny part where the green takes on a whitened hue.

I was running through the woods with my eyes half-closed and the strange sensation of feeling my bare feet on the grass and thorns. I was steadying myself to jump a fence, measuring the distance to make sure there was no danger. I suddenly felt frightened, sure I was going to bump into a tree trunk, feel pain in the middle of my face, bang my nose and be covered in red blood. I opened my eyes and saw Graciano.

'In these parts at this hour?'

'I'm going to the mayor's house, I have to talk to him.'

'Well, take the other way; this path peters out in the oak tree wood.'

Nobody passed by there in the early morning. After much twisting and turning, stony patches, and sudden landslide of lizards, the lane drops down past Mourence and into populated areas.

'What do you do in life, child?'

'Can't you see on my shoulders the tools of my trade?'

'Wouldn't you be better off studying?'

'Still studying, when I'm over twenty?'

'From what the storekeeper told me, you're no more than fifteen.'

HER FATHER HAD LEFT THEM eight hundred pesetas; that is, a few coins to share between her, her mother, her brother and sister. The boy spent his on a night of revelling with the errand boys in the bawdy quarter in Vilapedre.

The first thing I did was find a place to keep the pouch with my two hundred pesetas. Since our house boasted no cupboard or anything resembling one, or even a chest or trunk, I thought the best thing would be to hide it in the folds of my petticoat and take the coins out when I needed them.

THE VILLAGE WAS SMALL, I think that is very clear, with very few Christians, because Galicia is predominantly pantheistic. Encounters were longed for on the pathways and in the only store in the village, the one that Miragaya ran until his school prospered. The shop gave off a fragrance of cloves, burnt paper with candy sugar, good clean sweat, and jasmine flowers. Loliña was in and out because Graciano was always there.

'Give me a bunch of valerian, Señor Miragaya, to see if it calms my mother.'

'Here you are. Don't worry, my girl, you take after her. These ants in your pants must come from somewhere, take it from me because I don't like staying put either. And if I don't pack in the store now I'm the concierge, it's because I'm shackled to my trade.'

'Miragaya, give her a glass of Sansón too, it's good for the health.'

'You're too kind, Señor Graciano. Always looking out for me.'

'Why shouldn't I look, Loliña? You're a beauty. Don't you go to school? How old are you? And your mother, has she wed again?'

'What do you mean? That's what they do in other places. Here we care for our men to the very end and we're still faithful after death.'

GRACIANO BARELY LEFT the store. The smell reminded him of the sweets he used to steal from Chinaman Chang when he ran errands as a boy in Cuba. 'Don't go into Chang's shop,' Misia Saturna would warn him, 'the smoke is a sign of Lucifer's fire where sinners burn.' But he knew only too well that Señor Chang was doing no harm; he was in the back of the shop smoking opium from Hong Kong.

Graciano's father was called Marcelino. He had been a day labourer in Bayamo, and then a sergeant in the rebel army. He died in a confrontation with Spanish troops and his wife was left with the weapons discovered in the house on San Nicolás street. Because she was the weaker sex, or so they thought, they pardoned her and she died in the Morro prison.

'WHERE DOES THIS CHILD come from, Miragaya?' asked Graciano, now considering himself among the most fortunate of men.

'She's the daughter of the witch and *El Gateño*, also known as *El Cagadreito*, who died four years ago of tuberculosis. The little girl was ten then. She has worked for her mother ever since. She runs errands for her, milks the cows, grooms them... but don't go getting ideas that you're a mule with pert buttocks, Graciano, you must be storing up useless watery semen incapable of making a woman pregnant.'

LOLIÑA'S MOTHER was Manuela, daughter, granddaughter, great granddaughter of druid priestesses, who handed down their arts in Galicia through the female line. Manuela could tell the future without reading cards, soothe rheumatism with a few incantations, and cure animals with more skill than vets. She was from the village of La Redondela, so people called her *La Redondelana*. It was said she had no equal in hocus-pocus and all kinds of jiggery-pokery, and that Merlin himself would give her ten out of ten for cunning and wisdom.

Whoever says that is wrong. My mother had her destiny and her life. She used her arts to do what she wanted and walked a tightrope to survive. That was my mother.

The people who consulted her had long incurable illnesses that doctors did not know how to treat. Winter or summer, snow or shine, she always washed in dew. Sometimes she would lie with patients to teach them how to breathe: mouth to mouth, body to body, moving with them. She tried so many different tacks some of them had to work. She talked to people, massaged them until their temperatures dropped.

Many claimed she was blessed with the breasts of a young girl, and no one could guess her age.

The priest disapproved of her, and the villagers feared her, always frightened she would put the evil eye on them.

To cure sadness and the unknown maladies of donkeys, goats, cows, pigs and sheep, she would hang a scapular of San Blas round the animals' necks for a week and on their respective saints' days she prescribed a crust of holy bread.

Chapter Three

ONE MORNING GRACIANO just happened to pass Loliña's house in Los Rañegos. The path runs along the river. When it comes out onto a plain they call Pena de Miguel, it snakes around muddy pools until it reaches a log bridge where frogs regale passers-by with their diving.

The whole house was made of stone, with an upper floor and an attic. Sheep and cows sheltered on the ground floor, especially in winter when they hardly went out. The warmth of cooked turnips ascended the chimney.

I slept in an attic room which had a skylight right above the straw mattress. It was the hub of the house and the ceiling swarmed with mice. The best food was kept there, the bacon and the lard. When I had a fever as a child, my dreams knew no bounds. I took to spending an hour or more up there as night fell, standing on tiptoe watching the heavenly bodies; I could see an ant even on the darkest of nights.

'The witch's daughter nosing around in the stars!'

At night, the brightest stars soared and fell like glowing birds, more so when the whole of Lanzós was blacked out after a downpour.

'DON'T YOU THINK Loliña should study, Consuelito?'

'Good God! Where did you ever see a woman studying?'

'In Madrid they're already beginning, and in Paris. Even in Cuba... reading, writing, and then a young ladies career.'

'She'd be better off learning to sew like her grandmother, and embroider and knit. She could be a maid in some big house.'

It was extraordinary how prestigious knitting was: many young girls with ambition devoted themselves to it without giving up work in the fields. Their husbands, meanwhile, went off to reap the harvest in Castile, be bricklayers in Catalonia, or for good to the Americas.

AS WELL AS NOT BEING too good at washing clothes or domestic chores, Loliña did not find learning to read any easier. As was the custom, the school teacher began by teaching her the letters of the alphabet by a, b, and c. And Loliña replied, 'Ant, bee, and cow,' because that was how her mind worked naturally. So they sent her to learn sums with Miragaya in his tavern.

I tried to learn the four rules with him, but never got the hang of it. He taught me to add up on my fists: five and five make ten. I began with my fingers, one, two, three... but when I got to five with my thumb, I counted six with my pinky and always made nine. He shook his head, he didn't understand. More advanced arithmetic was worse. 'If there are this many litres of red wine in this barrel, how many will there be in that one?' Since I couldn't multiply either, he changed tack: 'All right, this barrel holds white wine, girl.'

SHE COULDN'T GET IT into her skull that while 'bough' was pronounced 'bow', 'cough' was not 'cow' but 'coff', and 'ought' was not 'out' but 'awt'. There was no logic to it, and she had to learn grammar in her own fashion. Singing in the parish choir every day got her ear attuned, and she learned to speak by listening, in the same way she could sing with no idea of scales.

At school they forced me to recite by heart for the nth time The Death of Prim, The Executions on the Andalucian Train, *or tales from places as far away and unimaginable as Ribadeo, Ponferrada or Mondoñedo: names which were common currency in the mouths of cattle dealers, weekly fish merchants, or itinerant cobblers, and aroused in me vague dreams of ambitions to travel the world.*

She spent her spare time learning the catechism. She knew the Ave Maria, the Salve Regina and also the names of the prophets, but it didn't help her disentangle the intricacies of the Trinity. Graciano, however, gave her *The Notary's Nose* (Edmond About),

Spring Loves (Alberto Insúa), and *Diary of a Hunter* (Miguel Delibes) to read. When she turned sixteen, he presented her with *Dead Souls*, and the adolescent would often sneak away to hear the melodramas blind men used to recite at fairs.

GRACIANO CAME BACK TO SEE CONSUELITO. Their mother neglected her daughters, absorbed as she was in matters to do with her craft. As the eldest daughter, Consuelito ran the house.

'There's no future in knitting, Consuelito. We *indianos* from La Habana want to help young people. Your sister will get the first scholarship. Nursing is...'

'Yes, yes, let her be a nun...'

'For God's sake! You can do good works without a wimple.'

'Well, I don't see any trade but sewing.'

'They've got a bad reputation...'

They would carry their belongings in baskets on their head, go to villages and stay with families who prepared a pile of sheets for them to mend or turn into knickers and underpants; torn tablecloths to make napkins; shirts with threadbare collars for sanitary towels, to be kept out of sight of children.

My sister inherited the housekeeping, so the witchcraft fell to me. Our mother made me stand beside her while she performed her rituals, and subconsciously I learned cures for all kinds of diseases, of body and of mind, as well as scaring away the Devil, rescuing souls from Purgatory, and driving out evil spirits.

'AREN'T YOU TIRED of working so hard, Miragaya?'

'You're lucky, Graciano, to be able to live off your savings.'

'How much would you get for the store?'

'Not enough to buy two cows.'

'I'll give you six for it.'

'I could see this coming, Graciano. I told you not to do anything rash, that girl will be the death of you. Can't you see your grey

23

hairs are telling you your grave beckons, and are already mourning your imminent end?'

'If only it were that easy! You're lucky you're so sensible. For me, if the sun comes out, I imagine she's the sun. And if by chance, I catch a glimpse of her from afar, all my blood drains from my body; I get delirious and can't sleep for at least a week.'

In the end, Miragaya gave up being a storekeeper; he exchanged the store for an apartment in town. Graciano put the shop in the name of Dolores Rego. He was determined to open a typical bazaar with goods from over the seas.

FOR THE VILLAGE it was a novelty, for its children a hall of wonders. They watched in amazement as Graciano stocked up with merchandise that in his childhood had filled the Chinaman's stall: Manila silk shawls, which in Cuba little rich boys gave to brothel girls to serve as bedspreads for extramarital prowess, but in Graciano's store they collected dust, cobwebs, and, with the humidity, soon looked like moth-eaten banners in a museum.

Fruit bowls from Bohemia that looked like carved ice were soon covered in a greasy crust of buzzing flies. There were sweets of all kinds, caramel-coated mouthfuls filled with papaya, and crystalline buttered molasses that the village folk pulled and kneaded with their fingers till it turned into elastic gum, like toffee.

AFTER SO MANY YEARS, it is only natural that the memory of many of the marvels in the bazaar has faded. But let us make an approximate tally, at least of those that have survived the journeys and waves of emigration, and passed the test of time, like the remains of a shipwreck in the bottom of a trunk.

On the first shelf was a row of bottles of Basbieta liqueur, a green liquid that cured every kind of ailment because of the pure and primary earth the water dragged with it down the solitary River Pedernel.

On the second were medicinal powders and ointments.

Camphor balls, to be hung in a bag around a girl's neck or placed in a boy's pocket, raised barriers no epidemic could overcome. Bars of ram's fat for inflammations, and chicken fat fried with oregano and bay leaves, which when heated cured hoarse voices, bronchitis and sore throats.

And on the last shelf, the magic of herbs: ivy for asthma and coughs; white pennyroyal for chest infections; and cinnamon from Ceylon for stomach cramps. Most miraculous of all the remedies were the properties of the hoopoe bird whose fat 'applied for memory loss' boasted the prospectus to 'bring back the past'; whose feathers which 'if stuck on a man who fights another, will win him the bout and his laurels'; whose cooked flesh 'cures colic' and its blood 'eliminates white spot in the eye'. If you sprinkle it on doves 'birds of prey don't come near'.

Loliña loved admiring the store from the street, amazed by the confusion of colours: the shop window full to brimming and the sign which Graciano had orientalised with his surname to make it look even more like Chang.

CHAO GROCERY STORE

Chapter Four

I COULD NEVER HAVE IMAGINED the immense joy I would feel when the bazaar was inaugurated. I understood that love is a passion we cannot jettison just because we want to; especially if it makes us suffer and stops us obeying reason.

Those two lovers, who had every right to consummate their passion, had been forced to practise the utmost amorous restraint. They were increasingly intoxicated by the frenzy that consumes hearts which share a secret. However, it is universally acknowledged that when two hearts seek, they find each other and unite despite the obstacles. So they managed to outwit the vigilance of the priest and Loliña's mother and calm their ever-alert suspicions. They put their trust in their natural instincts and delighted in their love. They spent that happy day flirting and exchanging glances, their lips together and their legs entwined. The young girl learned to love the old man more than eating with her fingers. When she offered him her body, she gave him her soul as well. For the first time, she realised the effect of unconditional love, the magnitude of which had never before crossed her mind.

My body had never known love before. It invaded my life, and with it came anxiety. I will never forget how I felt at that moment. It was as if the lukewarm contact between two beings turned into the penetrating heat of burning metal; or as if my hand, by caressing those ageing shoulders, rubbed granite soaked in melted snow.

For his part, the fortunate lover proved himself up to the task and returned her love in a manner miraculous for his age, making her feel the unimaginable. And in both their hearts, joy took the place of hope. They were deliriously happy for a time, loving each other more and more deeply, with each passing day. Graciano was very proud to see his little girl blossom into a beauty, and become more confident and lively.

Chao Grocery Store was a most tantalising vision. You could not look around without seeing enticing signs written in strange characters, from the enormous 'Emporium' sign hung on a wire across the street, to the small labels between the folds of materials: 'Pure linen!' 'From Ceylon!' 'Everything at two *reales*' 'Bargain!' 'Take your Pick' 'Something for Everyone: mittens, fans, tulle, tinsel, nun's veils, muslin, all at unimaginable prices.'

The baroque and grandiloquent advertising slogans came from the pen of the peerless Olegario, the town scribe, who found a target for his arsenal of quotes and anecdotes, taken from the interminable lurid novels in his library.

The baskets with bottles of liquor, fruit and groceries were never empty. Pleasure and joy guided every hour and moment of life. Farmhands stopped and stared, bewitched by such variety of colour. Scythe in hand, goat in tow, bundles of cabbages on their heads, their opinions wavered between astonishment and envy, both articulated by an exclamation the *indianos* brought back from Cuba.

'*Le zumba el mango!*'

The gossip was unanimous. Loliña had turned the head of a sexagenarian who could be her grandfather.

Dazed by such profusion of feelings, half inebriated by an ambiance infused with oriental fragrances, there was a touch of madness in the way Graciano opened his purse strings.

'Mad? Me? Because I use my money to live? Mad are they who stick it under the mattress, and don't even take it out for a bit of good incest.'

To cap it all, he sent to La Habana for a crescent-shaped portico like the one the Chinaman had 'fol see melchandise bettel'. Timber, transport, and glass reduced his assets further, not to mention the cost of the artisan brought from Barcelona to build it.

My memory of all the herbal cures has faded, but I still recall the respect with which any botanical ointment was received. It found pride of place in our apothecary, fraternising with the parsley mixed with alcohol and candy sugar that relieved rheumatism and even cured the bitter taste of injustice.

That corner of Cuba transferred to Lanzós was a true Amelia Peláez painting. At the sight of the multiple dancing colours of the fabrics blowing in the breeze, labourers stared open-mouthed, like tourists in front of the rose window of Chartres Cathedral. All the more so, because out of the nave soared celestial music, through the loudspeaker of the first His Master's Voice wind-up gramophone to be heard in Galicia.

'It's the devil's work!'

Belatedly and somewhat aggrieved, her mother went to see the altarpiece. True, her house was half a league from the shop, but also true was that the relationship between the Cuban and her daughter irritated her. More than ever now she was hearing such extravagant comments; she felt the need to see with her own eyes and ears, as they say.

If she had gone in the morning, her reaction might have been different. Before opening the shop, Loliña swept more or less properly in front of the door, tidied everything after a fashion, and took the goods out of the well, where they were kept overnight in the cool. However, as the day wore on, a sickly smell of decomposed mango, fermented mamey and the peel of rotten guava wafted out into the street. Filaments of tangled miasmas completed the afternoon scene. When night finally fell, the neighbourhood was awash with festering fruits macerated in their tropical stench.

'Holy God, how sinful!'

WHEN THE NOVELTY wore off and the visitors' amazement palled, nobody gave the Chao Grocery Store another glance; its decline began almost as soon as it opened.

'You'll see,' insisted Graciano. 'These country bumpkins are used to shrunken apples and rachitic pears from San Juan, they're not going to suddenly eat guava and mango. We have to get them used to these novelties.'

While she lay listlessly amongst the vegetables, he bankrupted himself importing exotic wares. The well was overflowing with merchandise that came all the way from Cuba only to be attacked by worms in the back of the shop. Even the animals turned up their snouts, and most of most of them were pigs.

A brilliant idea occurred to Graciano, however, after a short period of bickering and an immediate new outbreak of love.

'If those yokels don't come to the shop, we'll take it to their villages.'

No sooner saddled up, than off on the trail. An inner spring propelled him into the stable of Culitrenzado, an ass of lean flanks and broad nostrils, tamed by distant gypsies who had sheared his haunches in arabesque patterns and platted his tail. He had two saddlebags, one for barley, and one for chorizo for his fellow travellers. Phantom soliped, invisible shadow of improbable donkey as light of body as of movement, he stood on his four legs by a pure miracle of levitation and weighed so little that he left no trace on the ground. He appeared and disappeared like the clouds and the spirits of the Santa Compaña: an ascetic, a dream become bones; a fakir who lived by fasting, his only food served up by providence.

Despite his noisy tuberculosis and his evanescent decrepitude, he was used to pulling carriages and flew along like straw in the wind, spurred on by a flick of the whip.

In a corner of the shed stood the rusting passenger vehicle, green with red stripes, that Graciano got out for baptisms, weddings and funerals. That very same day, he dusted it off, greased the axles, and oiled the harnesses.

In those early days, the shadows that clouded the splendour of my feelings did not worry me. Graciano was an affectionate companion, and our love was consolidated in the intimacy of our walks, hand in hand under the vines. A pity that sometimes nerves do not easily submit to the forces of reason!

Chapter Five

WHAT A CARNIVAL THE VILLAGERS put on at the sight of their very first cavalcade! A crowd from all over the county gathered in the main square, attracted by this magnificent and unusual spectacle. Young people came dressed in luxurious multicoloured clothes and wearing their grandmothers' jewellery, which knowledgeable souls valued at several measures of bran, and even then they thought they had underestimated.

The procession set off. Leading it, were two bands. Barely stopping for breath, they blew out their cheeks as they tried to get the music right on their metal mouthpieces. In front of the donkey walked twelve children dressed as slaves, in two rows of three, one on the right and one on the left. Two held the ribbons attached to the caparison. The rest brought up the rear. Following them, came groups of villagers, and also some outsiders, all in typical local dress.

Culitrenzado dropped his ears a little to look at himself in the puddles. He advanced along the riverbank moving his head from side to side with aplomb, with no fear of mistaking the way. He would take his time, because slow is the pace of a donkey often led down bad paths (after all, what abbess or clergyman ever mounted a donkey?). Now and then, a mule would come up to him, attracted by the smell of the quadruped. But he, whom all the young colts of the Sancobad hills had not persuaded to take a wrong turning, received them with bared teeth and bridle, without altering his pace.

At first I got up in the driver's seat under the awning. I was astonished to see a beast of burden so intuitive and sure of itself. I told Graciano to use the reins and he laughed in a Cuban sort of way:

'Don't be silly, Loliña. Culitrenzado doesn't need anyone to tell him where to head for!'

THE REAR PART OF THE WAGON sported shelves stacked with bunches of herbs and drawers full of spices. On the counter, covered with a cloth, stood medicinal plants – celandine, euphorbia, marshmallow, hollyhock and the seven herbs of Umbanda to combat envy – and lots of bottles containing all sorts of ointments and elixirs. To cap it all, Graciano put an astrolabe on the counter and dressed up like an oriental fortune teller.

Seeing the splendiferous carriage and the elegant donkey make their entrance was quite a sight. The whole village rushed to admire the graceful Loliña and the novel merchandise. As they flocked to the elaborate stall, Culitrenzado began braying to the four winds and the echo attracted a multitude of local farm workers. Although the sound might not have been to the taste of music lovers, avid as they are for harmony, it was appreciated in certain quarters. Despite its dissonance, farmers recognised Culitrenzado's way of expressing his amorous longings; he was hungry for love after his long journey, and that hunger inspired respect. And like any good male, his cry was much more plaintive than the female of the species. The men of the county tried borrowing his braying for their own amorous declarations, as had been the case in the past: from some of Pliny's writings we can see that in Roman amphitheatres men were hired to imitate braying. While they may have been the first to discover the art of braying, others would perfect it as Apuleius recounts in the *Golden Ass* and Cervantes in his *Don Quixote*.

In vain they did not bray
Both the mayors, they

Graciano stepped onto the wagon in his mandarin disguise. With his impressive voice, he gathered the populace around him with amazing promises:

'There is no illness however grave, be it leprosy, bubonic plague, or scarlet fever, even in its death throes, that cannot be cured by smelling excrement.'

By the time he finished his humbug, hundreds were convinced. His fame spread like wildfire. Candidates of every class and condition began to descend on him. He listened to them and prescribed hazardous treatments.

His audience crowded round the carriage. They brought him urine and excrement; he sniffed and proclaimed his medical verdict: 'The distinguished owner of this defecation has such and such an ailment.' The patient, taken in by the vagaries of the gobbledygook, thought, 'It is true. By the holy saints my illness is this and not the other.'

He examined any old halfwit and always found the key to his troubles:

'You there, I can see you're a inquisitive fellow, it has come to my ears that you're very troubled by a certain part of your body that isn't functioning and that many physicians have tried to cure, but cannot. But we will cure you, my man, without giving you drugs or applying ointment upon ointment.'

'Cure me and I will make you rich, and your children and your children's children. I'll shower you with favours and mercies; whatever I have is yours. You will be my friend and my guest. Restore to my ears, for pity's sake, the sharpness that has abandoned them! What will you do, by the Virgin of Remedios, to give me back my hearing?'

'My father is Chinese, and I've read the sacred books from seven generations back; books by sages about the fundaments of knowledge. I know the patterns of the stars, verses by educated men, and I have studied all the sciences until I know more than the most erudite scholars of my time. My name is famous for a myriad of treatments, and my fame has spread to many lands. There is no corner of the globe that news of me has not reached.'

It was not long before the locals turned up with sick animals, women afflicted with imaginary curses, crippled children, and even limbless men who hoped their nether parts would grow with products from the wild.

BUSINESS WAS GOING SO WELL that Graciano, with his nose for a commercial opportunity, decided to turn one of his assistants into a dentist, a trade he considered very profitable given the number of cavities he had himself. He offered the job to Pumariño with whom he used to search the hills and ravines for precious plants and hunt toads and snakes. His diminutive name belied his robust arm.

Any visitor to the fair from whom Pumariño extracted teeth was either a hero or candidate for a madhouse. The village odontologist did his best, but his best was to sit the patient in a barber's chair, strap his head back, open his mouth, wedge in a piece of wood, and extract the appropriate tooth with a pair of pliers. The victim bellowed, roared, tried to escape that inquisitorial torment, but after X attempts Pumariño managed to uproot it together with various bits of gum. Sometimes he made a mistake, and instead of picking the rotten molar, he struggled with the neighbouring one. And that was the apotheosis: herbs and potions flew in all directions, and the poor operative had to be rescued from the patient's ire by the good offices of the forces of law and order.

MIRAGAYA HAD WARNED THEM: 'Tread with caution, Graciano. Use your wealth wisely and don't swindle anybody, because fortune isn't eternal and prosperity ends when fate decrees it.'

But it was too late. Intoxicated by his fortune and anxious to make more, Graciano asked his friends in La Habana to send a pot of ointment that would put him on a par with the gods. They refused, but so persistent was he that one day the jar arrived accompanied by a letter warning of its adverse effects. 'Take note that this ointment is the work of occult forces, which have given it supernatural powers. Suffice it to apply a little round the left eye and on the eyelid, for the anointed eye to see the places where all the treasures of the world lie buried. But if by chance it is applied to the right eye, both eyes will immediately be blinded.'

ARRAYED IN LUCUMBA FINERY, one day Graciano announced with great solemnity that Elegguá himself had sent him a remedy with extraordinary powers. He only had one jar, at an enormous price, because it was unique and divine. He put the price so high that although everyone searched their pockets, nobody approached the platform.

He noticed in one group of spectators, a famished-looking young man, consumed by some sickness that left him resembling a wrinkled wineskin without wine. The high price of the treatment disheartened the poor man. He said so with the confused Ciceronian grandiloquence that was beginning to affect everybody and made his phrases impenetrable.

'You know all too well that a man of my birth cannot permit himself to squander such an amount of money to restore my health. If you only knew how long I have been waiting to emerge from my misfortune! But it is written that I must drink the cup of infelicity down to the dregs.'

Each week Graciano raised the price of the merchandise. The higher the price, the more the onlookers desired it, until that Friday the crowd reached gigantic numbers. Among them was a judge, not too bright but renowned for his fortune and ambition. He listened attentively to the speechifying about the product's improbable powers and about which thousands of claims had been made: that it made dwarfs grow, put feet on limbless men, and gave sight to the blind from birth. After much haggling, Graciano agreed to apply the ointment to the judge. But he warned him in all honesty that he could only put it on one eye; putting it on the two might make him blind.

The judge did not need asking twice. He leapt onto the

platform. Graciano took his money with theatrical parsimony, took a tiny bit of the balm on the tip of his finger and started to rub it on the left eye.

'Open your eyes, wise sheriff, look out of the left and close the right. Tell us what you see.'

After a few unbearable minutes waiting for the ointment to take effect, the guinea pig began:

'Normal objects fade away and a series of superimposed planes appear made up of underground and underwater grottos, and in them enormous trees with caves in their roots, chambers carved in the rock and hiding places of huge proportions. All are filled with treasure chests overflowing with precious stones, gems, jewels, and coins of all colours, shapes and sizes. And in the mines, I see virgin silver, crystals and gold ingots, and seams of precious metals so large they encircle the earth.'

On seeing all that treasure, this judge of morality wanted to pounce on the first piles of jewels with the speed of a falcon on a dove. But by coveting so many marvels, his eye got tired. He could not restrain himself, and opened the other one. At that very instant, his sight returned to rest on the ladies and gentlemen of the audience, the wizard and the donkey, who was not in the least surprised.

The judge was the most perplexed; he did not know what to think. He said to himself: 'This charlatan Chinaman is a fraud and only proved so affable to trick me, because it cannot be that the same product has such different effects under the same conditions just by changing eyes. Doubtless he now wants me now to pay triple what he first asked.' And addressing Graciano he said with the type of smile that in Galicia we call *suiña,* that is, false, twisted:

'Maestro, my friend, it seems you wished to mock me by what you said, because I cannot believe a substance can have such opposite effects. I think applying it to the right eye will put at my disposal that treasure my left eye showed me. What do you say to that? Have you ever experimented with the ointment in both eyes? Don't beat about the bush, because I warn you that come what may, I want to see for myself. So apply it to me, and don't try to cheat me because it could cost you dear.'

The pomade seemed to have contaminated the speech and the actions of both the audience and the judge's wife.

'Careful, husband, remember that if you put your trust in this charlatan you risk the worst of all fates, because no matter how much money you give him, he will always try to cheat you. Can't you see he has bewitched you with a medicinal mixture made by African negroes? Who knows if it works the same on Galician justices?'

'Quiet, faintheart! I am prepared to face my fate with courage! I will accept it with a brave heart. Do your worst! Bring it on!'

'This request is unwise and dangerous,' insisted Graciano. 'I cannot agree to do you harm after having done you so much good. Do not be so insistent as to force me to do something you will probably regret all your life. Let us part as good friends and go our own ways.'

There were some fifty or sixty souls there and triple that number of flies. From the former not a single intake of breath was to be heard, from the latter only the rustling of wings. The silence was broken in any case by the huffing and puffing of the pettifogger, convinced that the aim of the charlatan's remonstrations was merely to keep the treasure. Moreover, he had used him as a guinea pig to test the ointment and the amount of the treasure so that he could keep all of it for himself. He stood facing him:

'Zounds, on your mother's head! I'm warning you that if you don't put the cream on my other eye, I will pursue you with the full force of the law for the rest of your life.'

Graciano turned very pale and his face took on a hard look no one had seen before. He grabbed the pot angrily:

'Mark my words, señor, you are going to blind yourself of your own free will.'

The flies disappeared. The only sound now was the judge's

wife sobbing with terror before she managed to faint or simulate a blackout.

Graciano smeared a handful of ointment over the justice's right eye and eyelid.

'The treasure has disappeared. Now I see rocks and stony ground, deserts and ice caps. The sun is hiding behind a huge cloud and everything is covered in darkness, there is a shaft of lighting and now a clap of thunder.'

From that moment on, the judge saw only darkness before both his eyes. When he realised he was blind, he came to his senses and, perplexed and imploring, held out his arms to the swindler without knowing in which direction:

'Babylonian sorcerer! Don't you think it a sin that in three minutes you have taken away my sight? Deliver me from this darkness!'

'In truth, brother, your tale is rare and holds a goodly lesson. As the saying goes, "He who doth not consequences weigh, will always live to rue the day." Was Your Honour not warned? Consider now that the punishment is a purifying fire and trust that life's reverses open the eyes of those who are born blind.'

The righteous lawmaker returned to uttering all kinds of threats, ones that would terrify those not blessed with oriental patience.

'What good would it do to punish me like that?' went on Graciano with apparent innocence. 'Those who wish to outrun their shadows, run in vain; it is futile to try and abate an echo with shouts louder than ones that produced it. You yourself are to blame for what happens to you. But bear in mind that it was already decreed in ages past by the Creator and all predictions must be fulfilled for each and every one of us to realise our destiny. Astrologists must surely have told your father when you uttered your first cries: "Countless calamities will befall your son!" Now what was prophesied has come to pass. So, the only choice before you now is patience until the Almighty turns your pain to joy, since it is written that the greater the suffering, the greater the reward.'

The judge had to bow to the evidence before him.

'There is truth in what you say. But now tell me what I must learn and where I must direct my steps.'

The newly sightless man heard Graciano click his tongue at Culitrenzado and rapidly leave the fair. He fell to the ground and was unconscious for a long time. He would surely have died of grief and bewilderment right there if someone had not sought out the fair's resident blind man who went round the villages singing ballads about criminal acts. Like all good colleagues, he promised the judge he would teach him to sing and scratch the violin for a living. What he could not provide was a blind man's guide, much less a female like the one he had.

To make matters worse, the blind man's wife abandoned him in his plight, because to be labelled blind meant a stain on her noble lineage and a considerable decline in her social standing. Nevertheless, this new member of the blind fraternity began to study grammar with the local troubadour, and became an expert in the discipline. He began a life as a poet and musician, without giving a thought to the future; trusting everything to fate and the Lord of all creatures, who is endlessly indulgent.

He wrote a fair number of ballads, many of which people still sing today. Even so, he was reduced to the fate befalling all blind beggars: if you sing nobody listens, if you don't sing you starve to death.

Chapter Six

PRIESTS, DOCTORS, animal doctors and even doctor animals joined forces to demand the expulsion of that trio of pedlars who pulled out healthy teeth, blinded justice and, to cap it all, took the bread out of their mouths.

For country people, it fell to the doctor with his fortuitous science to succeed the secular knowledge of the quack. The haughty physicians were more than ready to wrest from the Church the job of guiding consciences; they took over modern society like the clergy did with the previous superstitious one, imposing the yoke of rationalism on new generations of hypochondriacs and neurasthenics, just as God-fearing people had suffered Christian dogma.

Sumptuous clinics and laboratories appeared, the edifices replacing the cells the monasteries were blessed with. Doctors took over from the Jesuits in giving intimate advice to society ladies. More importance was placed on a medical consultation than on confession. And almost nobody believed in the Devil any more, only in microbes. Soon the religion of hygiene would triumph, beginning the glorious reign of asepsis and antisepsis. Prophylaxis would finally save humanity from pain and ignorance, and assure the social supremacy of doctors over priests.

The pedlars were denounced because they had blinded the judge, whereas previously it was justice that was blind. Some patients were left with no dentures but had they not bitten Pumariño as well? And a lot of animals had kicked the bucket in fits of agony after herb cures, but who had forced farmers to give their pigs daisies? Those unfortunate souls – men and beasts – would probably have met the same fate anyway. No one can be sure that the most secret of joys be always safe from the prying eyes of malcontents and gossips. Nonetheless, our couple and the tooth-puller, no disrespect to the ass which like all his species had therapeutic gifts (remember 'Memoirs of the Illustrious Ass Academy' by Cristóbal Serra where braying is said to produce the same effect as a purge), were expelled from all the county fairs.

So, poor Loliña and Graciano had to take refuge in their store in Lanzós once again.

With this disaster our whole world collapsed. I was so sick of life that death seemed preferable. I was used to being out and about with Graciano, and we were known the length and breadth of the county, so a dozen hovels and a hundred local yokels was small beer for me now. The only thing I relished was taking the cows to pasture, but they soon tired of it and stood there with that gormless inaccessible gaze, all-knowing, with stubborn illusions and inscrutable horizon, as if read once and engraved forever.

Worse still, one day when Loliña was with her animals the civil guard arrived. Her age? Fifteen. And quick as a flash, these lecherous (and shrewd) policemen said they had already arrested Graciano. They released her because she was a minor. But, out of jealousy, they took Graciano to court in Irimia and questioned him about witchcraft, corruption of minors, competing with vets, healers, quacks and other charlatans.

LOLIÑA TOOK FRIGHT and decided to run away, but not before saying goodbye to Miragaya (in whom she had confided her forebodings) and asking for his blessing. It was the custom in Galicia to give travellers advice before their journey. The story was told of a father who asked his son to get onto the table and throw himself into his arms for their last embrace. The boy did so and, as he flew through the air, his progenitor opened his arms in an amorous gesture (like the Christ of Lepanto), and the boy fell flat on his face.

'Son, that will teach you to trust no one, not even your father.'

The good Miragaya tried to dissuade her. Like a prophet of doom, he insisted that her disappearance would be the death of her beloved adoptive grandfather.

'Forget the idea, please, it is foolish. The most senseless thing you can do is to risk your life for no good reason. Listen, child, I've never seen a star steer such a narrow course in the zodiac as in these past months. The firmament shows tomorrow as an ill-fated day and the day after even worse; I'm afraid something terrible will happen. So, I think you'd better wait for a more propitious time for your journey. Stay here until the planets are aligned again.'

But Loliña proved stubborn. All hope of persuading her lost, Miragaya assumed his patriarchal role and started dusting off the *Arcane Book of Farewells* to recite the strict instructions with considerable pomposity.

'I am resigned to accept what you decide because fate and destiny control the moon, the sun and the eclipses. If they see fit, they blindfold the eyes of human beings. Nevertheless, child, I think it fitting to remind you what wise men who shape our behaviour say: 'Who so much as embarks on an enterprise without considering its serious nature, is but a child.'

'I want to recommend several things, dear Loliña,' Miragaya went on, all priest-like, holding the book in front of him.

'First, don't get too close or familiar with anybody, avoid anyone who might bring you trouble and sorrow, and be on your guard against bad people, since as the poet said…' he thumbed the pages:

A secret plague are men;
Never put your trust in them.
If you give them your heart
They will very soon depart.

'They're like blacksmiths. If his fire doesn't burn you, his smoke will suffocate you. So steer clear of anxiety and setbacks, security lies in maintaining a distance from the crowd, as another poet

said… it escapes me for the moment…' He looked in the index…
and finally said:

> *Talking to men is of no interest to you*
> *Unless to pass the time you do.*
> *Do not be close, I emphasise*
> *Except to learn, if they are wise.*

'Second, do ill to no one, so that good fortune smiles on you. Because in this world, luck may be with you or may be with your enemy, and all the good things in this life are but lent to you, and you will have to give them back some day.

'Third, learn to keep your counsel in society and concentrate on your own failings, not on the failings of others, because as the refrain says "security resides in silence", in other words as the Jesuits say "still waters run deep".

'Four, abstain from wine. And I say this as a former tavern keeper. Wine is the mother of all vices. It makes a mockery of friendship and blurs good judgement. So I insist, and I repeat, do not mix your drinks, because as the poet rightly says…' It took him several minutes to find what the poet had said…

> *By the gods, who urge so much good,*
> *Wine I must not try, just stick to food.*
> *Wine is treacherous, deceitful to youth,*
> *I like people who always tell the truth.*

'And my exhortation, the fifth, is twofold. Swear before God you will never frequent your countrymen to excess, nor give hospitality in your house except to strangers who are passing through. Experience teaches that a brief effusive encounter is preferable, by far, to a long friendship which can end badly. And if you are careful with your money, it will look out for you. Do not squander or misuse your property so you don't have to beg or be reduced to the most miserable of circumstances. So, save your pesetas, spend them prudently and do not take them to the grave. Be sure that in this world there is no better balm for open wounds, as the Arabic poet said…' He thumbed through various pages with his saliva-covered finger without finding the poet's name… 'I mean the anonymous poet…' before reciting:

If you spend your life making money
And all other pleasures eschew,
When you are old, what use
Will such money have been to you?

After talking to her like this and filling her head with such complicated instructions, Miragaya took his leave of a Loliña marvelling at the knowledge of the new school concierge. She did not sleep all night, memorising all the advice he had given her.

The next day finally dawned and as it wore on, Loliña practised to the letter all her patron's instructions. It was not long before she had achieved even more than she had hoped. However, the worst was still to come: saying goodbye to her mother. Would she dare or would she just vanish? She decided to confront it. Her mother responded impassively, as a clairvoyant would be expected to.

'How right you are, daughter, in what you have decided, although by my life, it pains me greatly to see you leave our land and your friends. Separation brings cause for reflection and a warning to the mild in spirit to be on their guard. I will say no more, I can be vexing. Wise men rightly say: "Keep your own counsel until you are asked and keep your nose out of what does not concern you, for you will not be thanked."'

Comforted by such good wishes, I departed in weather so damp it softened my bones. I took a long look at the house. I wanted a clear picture of it in my memory. Dark and sad, it was the house where I was born on the fifteenth of February in the year one thousand eight hundred and eighty. Many do not know the date they came into the world, but my mother knew my day all too well because according to her calculations, an intersection of two stars predicted it would happen.

Chapter Seven

TAKING HER SAVINGS FROM HER petticoat pocket, she set off with a few personal belongings and a notebook where Graciano (still behind bars) kept his addresses.

She went on foot from Lanzós to Irimia, as she had done many times before to attend country fairs. She headed for the Biscay hostel and asked if there was work in exchange for a bed for two nights and food. There she met a confectioner from Ferrol who was coming to a spa for a change of air, as they say, to cure his tuberculosis. Doctors used to say Irimia's benign climate was as good for the health as the potions they prescribed. Charmed by the girl's sweet nature, the confectioner offered to take her as far as Guitiriz in his carriage. He was going to the resort for fifteen days to drink litres of sulphuric water (worse than rotten eggs) to ward off hepatitis. For liver infections and rheumatic pains, which also plagued the confectioner, Loliña recommended *guacamaya* flowers to calm his bowels.

I would have liked to have got intimate with the pastry cook, because I adore sweets, and I could have my fill of that unbeatably delicious puff pastry they make pies with. How jealous my sister would be; watching me get fat and rosy with rounded curves from all that dripping. But I thought better of it.

ON THE OUTSKIRTS OF IRIMIA, the path forks at the foot of a mountain. One of the paths crosses the mountain, rising very steeply to the top. As fate would have it – no one escapes what is written – Loliña's steps lead her over the high road, which was four days and four nights hard-going to reach Guitiriz where the land levels out. On the way, she wandered into some rambling gardens which had belonged to the Sotomaior family and by the look of her muddy legs had got stuck in the quagmire.

The road from Guitiriz to Betanzos was another whole day in the San Fernando wagon, part riding in it, part walking beside it. She slept at a farm called Las Casillas after dining on some leftover omelette. When the next day dawned, she was tempted to retrace her steps and return to Lanzós. But she did not, because of her desire to seek new worlds. The ozone smell of the river spurred her on and her step quickened over the bridge.

Men started to pry with an insensitivity that disgusted me: especially the lewd expressions of the old ones. I could not understand that men who should inspire respect in me would ogle a young girl still with long hair down her back and petticoats half way up her legs. That's what they looked at, my legs. It was the first thing that attracted the pastry cook. He said he found me very appetising, even if I wasn't a jam roll. I began to understand that all men were pigs, and it was best to stay away from them. What would that gentleman have done with me in a hostel room in the dark? He'd have given me tuberculosis! Those thoughts made it impossible for me to act naturally or have a disinterested friendship, and they forced me always to be on the defensive.

WHEN GRACIANO CAME OUT OF PRISON, the wretched man could not stop wailing and cursing his luck. His neighbours came and told him, amid general ribaldry that, discontented with her lot, Loliña had gone away, taking what was left of their household. Nobody knew where she had gone, but they assumed it was to a country far away.

On hearing this, the good man understood the magnitude of his misfortune. Annoyed by the taunts and jokes everyone was making at his expense, he decided to leave the village straightaway. And so he did, without giving it a backward glance.

LA CORUÑA IS A MAGNIFICENT CITY bathed in light from four sides and smelling of brine and tar. The sea soon made its presence felt.

Before reaching the port, I realised that out there, on the other side, with no land in between, was Labana. It felt so close I could smell it, although later on I understood that the stench came from the tobacco factory and the dead fish on the dock. My heart broke at the thought of leaving my land. But there, over there, I would no longer be a little girl. I could walk openly with Graciano and sell herbs in the stores of some old Chang.

She spent that night wandering round the city, as if she were lost. Along streets, through squares, she dodged the teeth of dogs who wanted her gone from their domain. They pursued her like an intruder until dawn finally broke and she thought she had better find a safe place to hide. The docks were her ultimate refuge.

At seven that morning, I watched a transatlantic mail ship cut through the mist and arrive in the port. I did not know the name of the steamer, nor did I know where it was from or where it was going. I didn't care. That spectacle, together with the majesty of the horizon, filled my imagination with an even greater desire to cross the seas.

The ship entered the bay. She could not distinguish the passengers leaning on the rails of the deck because the ship was lit up and the lights blurred everything.

I suppose the sight of that illuminated ship was commonplace at that hour. But that day, amid the hustle and bustle, the noise of the crowd, the irresponsibility that hope gave me, my desire to sail somewhere spurred me on, to be an eternal passenger on one of those great, white illuminated liners.

SHE ASKED FOR THE PENSION ORENSANA in Los Olmos Street. The address was in Graciano's book. She pretended he had sent her.

'Yes, that's me, Maragato. Come in, my girl.'

As if he knew her. 'At your service,' he said, and he took her along a series of apparently deserted passageways. He introduced her to Maestro Chané, who had taken his choir on a tour through Europe, even to Albacete and Paris, and then been stripped of his chair at the School of Fine Arts in La Coruña. Now Curros

Enríquez had invited him to La Habana to set up a Galician colony choir. Chané offered to take her with him in a steamer that was leaving in three days time.

He had a second-class ticket worth four hundred pesetas. A fourth-class ticket for the two of us would be the same price. I don't know how much that was in reales, *because I never knew how to change notes into coins.*

The maestro took her into a back room of the Orensana where there was a piano. He wanted to try her out with a bit of warbling to see if she could join the company.

'What did you say the song was called?'

"*Unha noite na eira do trigo*', a poem of Curros's set to music that will have its debut on our opening night.'

He obviously liked me, because I was good at church canticles. Remarkable: the maestro confirmed he would arrange for me to board the ship, the Marqués de Comillas, *as his assistant.*

The port inspector, who was a bit of a crook, turned a blind eye and they falsified her date of birth.

You had to have your wits about you to stop these officials robbing you. And even so, they exploited people with this business of permits. The office was a beehive. It was sad to see so many young men with black berets and dreams of success in the colonies. And frightening to think they might not all fit in the very small island that Cuba looked in the atlas. The pen-pusher studied the papers, read the letters... tac, tac, tac, stamped the documents, this much to pay, and straight to the boat with papers in order. He did not even have time to look up.

A hundred metres from the hostel, at the entrance to the dock, was a ramshackle lean-to. It looked like a wasp's nest. Parents were saying goodbye to their sons, with sweethearts and sisters weeping; it was a real vale of tears.

No one was there to bid me farewell. Who would risk it for a fugitive? I was filled with doubts. I was braving the sea of anxiety for the first time. I did not even go through with Chané. We thought it better to go in separately. I was alone, and my village a long way away. What with the waiting, the hunger, and the sores on my feet, I have horrible memories of that crowd. At first sight, the sea looked bigger than the land. Perhaps because it is flat, you can see forever. And the boat, although enormous, was but a dot in the middle of so much water. The sea is infinite. That is why there are so many shipwrecks.

Chapter Eight

HERE BEGINS THE ADVENTURE of Loliña's first voyage in a big, tall steamship, which dances on the water and leaves a trail of sperm whales and flying fish in its wake. She does not know if the queasiness caused by the boat's rocking is in her mind or actually real. She sheds a fearful tear. Yet the bitter aftertaste in her mouth is sweetened by Chané's veiled concern:

'Do you feel seasick, Loliña?'

Consoling words and loving arms embrace her and calm her anxiety.

'It's nothing, dear. A bit of seasickness because of the vibration, that's all. When the engine stops, it will pass.'

IT IS WORTH DESCRIBING the crossing, one of the many thousand in those days. Third class was already a luxury for Galicians, second more than comfortable, and first a mere dream reserved for *indianos*. In fourth class, however, the bedbugs and fleas were better fed than the women and children crammed in with them.

We were thrown all topsy-turvy into the hold. After crossing themselves at the sound of the ship's siren, several emigrants started to harangue Chané. I discovered strange words and names I had never heard before. While I dozed, the talk around me was of levantiscos, maniguas, bohíos, Tagalog, and mambises, words as unfamiliar to me as the names of Martí, Maceo and Rizal. I did not know why they deserved such vile insults, but the subject of the colonies seemed to obsess everyone from the time they left port – not just until the Canary Islands, but all the way to Labana.

They wanted to put her to work. But doing what? At the store she had learned to write her name (badly). She could read, and loved it. Miragaya had taught her to add and subtract, of sorts. Apart from that, she knew how to take cows to graze and other country chores. So for the three hundred and seventeen hours of the crossing, she was stuck in a corner as an expert in gouging out potato eyes, peeling thousands of them and disposing of the rotten ones.

Thanks to a certain Benigno, I ate bread and chocolate. We sat together and he told me of the fiancée he had left behind, and so on and so forth. I remembered Miragaya's advice: 'Flies don't enter a closed mouth.' Especially if your shoulders are carrying a sin as big as mine.

Chané's beard was spongy, and his arms strong from conducting a hundred voices. She was better off there than in the softest bed. She slept in his embrace and for the first time realised what it was to have a good friend.

Impregnated with oil, limbs numb from being permanently doubled up, the hold passengers found it hard to keep their composure. A leg would suddenly stretch more than it should, a head fell on an adjacent shoulder, a little girl tried to sleep between her parents and Chané, indifferent to his neighbours' speechifying: 'Pursued tenaciously by the Spanish forces, rebel groups can only flee; burning and plundering as they go. They are more demoralised and dispersed by the day, with less and less incentive to continue their miserable attacks. The numbers of tired or repentant rebels surrendering and accepting pardons have increased since our heroic soldiers inflicted major setbacks on them.'

Tired of bellicose rhetoric and exploits, Chané undid his belt rather indecently, a sign of his unconditional surrender to the tyranny of the voyage.

I wanted to be sick. Hunger was increased by the sea breeze from the deck and the salt. The food was terrible. Almost always lentils or belly pork with bread and a glass of watery Madeira wine. But despite the creaking of the bunks, the bugs, the hum of the engines, and my desire to vomit, that boat was one big party.

As they passed the Azores, Chané's garrulous neighbour had the cheek or naivety to comment how tiring the sedentary position was; that's the word he used. Instead of laughing out loud, Chané murmured an incomprehensible monosyllable and returned to straightening his moustache, hostile yet apathetic to the stranger whom fate had forced him to endure on this interminable voyage.

No matter how often they would tell us we were still three or four days out, we all wanted to sight land. During the day our only distraction was going up on deck to watch the waves. How beautifully the sea breaks across the bows.

One morning some so-called doctors vaccinated her. During the voyage there was a daily check to see if there were any sick people or stowaways on board. So by the end of the voyage they had all had a thorough overhaul, although this vaccination was only against tropical illnesses.

Between seasickness, the smells and the fever I got from the vaccination, I spent the final days half asleep. I was told we had spied Cuba. I rushed out to see but thought it wasn't true, that I was still dreaming.

As they got near La Habana, they were all so shattered by the long days on board ship that their spirits hit rock bottom, a sign that all anyone wanted was to get off the boat, or do anything at all as long as the journey was over. Everyone was tired of talking, and had been since long before the Sargasso Sea.

From far away the island looked wonderful. The majesty of nature only palled when she saw the hundreds of ragged barefoot workers in inhuman conditions on the dockside. The waters round the steamer swarmed with native canoes filled with vendors competing to sell bananas, plantains and oranges. They put them in baskets and hauled them up to the passengers by rope.

The parrot finally stopped talking, because although he was prone to rhetoric he was not stupid. He was just as anxious to get on dry land and head for his hostel as the rest.

They finally docked amidst a forest of canoes and ropes.

'This is Labana,' said Lolita in ecstasy.

'No. La Habana.'

'Ah, La Bana. Like La Cruña?'

'That is the world', concluded Chané. 'Or rather, the world is worse, because, thank the gods, La Habana is not so corrupt, although people who have not been to Cuba talk of its immorality.'

Arrivals should always be happy; we have enough sadness with goodbyes. But this arrival was worse than any goodbye because it started pouring down and night was falling. I have never liked downpours. I prefer drizzle.

Chapter Nine

'STOP THINKING ABOUT HER, Graciano. Your heart is broken, but be grateful they didn't let you rot in jail.'

'I can't forget her. What will have happened to her? She probably got frightened and went to the brothels of the Rinconada in Lugo, or the Pombal in Santiago, or who knows, even to the Carrer d'Avinyó in Barcelona. Who with...?'

Sitting with a glass of *oruxo* telling the same old story, the days spent in the company of Miragaya were endless for Graciano. He had come back to Lanzós to settle a few problems of inheritance and debts. This business, being drunk, and thinking about her, were more than adequate pastimes.

'*Oruxo* has saved Galicians from freezing to death. It is the real patron saint of Galicia. If you're sad, it cheers you up; if you're happy, it makes you a bit bitter. If I was asked what I missed most about Galicia in Cuba, I would say a glass of *oruxo* and corn bread.'

'Look after the school, Graciano. The village loved you for your generosity, now no one gives you the time of day.'

'Ah, my dear Miragaya, I cannot bear the thought of losing her. So I will leave and think up a way to find her. I must succeed.'

'And how will you do it without being discovered?'

'I'll disguise myself as a merchant.'

To get rid of him, the new judge offered him an advantageous deal. He cleared his months-worth of grappa debt, bought a ship's passage, and still had a thousand *pesetas* to travel the world looking for his Loliña.

The rest fell to rack and ruin save the Chao Grocery Store, the ruins of which remained intact among brambles and melancholic sighs.

Chapter Ten

THE QUEUE MOVED SLOWLY. Three solitary inspectors checked the documents of thousands of immigrants, drenched by the downpour. People waiting on the quayside shouted out the names of new arrivals, who bellowed back from the rails down below. Lolita stepped out through a small iron door into dirty narrow streets where various men, who in terms of cleanliness were not much better than the streets, were unloading jerked beef from carts that others were loading up with sugar.

I will never forget my first impression of Labana. Not a bit like Lacruña. Low houses, almost non-existent pavements and famished-looking people.

They passed through an alley lined with bags of flour piled high above their heads and mountains of boxes of pasta. Under a tarpaulin lay a pile of sacks, barrels, boxes of all sizes, pitchers, rails, flagons, jars… Suddenly Lolita recoiled in terror. In front of her, yelling, 'Out of my way, out of my way,' strode a centaur, a satyr, or whatever that strange being made of pitch was.

'What race of monkey is that, Señor Chané?'

'It's not a "that". He's a coloured man.'

The existence of such beings was my grandmother's biggest surprise on disembarking. She had never seen one in her village, yet in the port of La Habana there were hundreds.

One stroked my head and I shook my hair for ages in case the colour came off his hand.

'We're black; we're men, not monkeys. We have hearts.'

'What a shock. That man read my thoughts.'

'Bah! He must be a *santero*.'

'What's that?'

'Like a magician who predicts everything.'

'Something like my mother?'

SHE REALISED THAT APART FROM Chané's protection, she had no letter of presentation, or any experience of any type of work. To whom, where, should she turn? She could not count on the maestro forever. Through these pedestrian streets and alleyways, sweaty men jostled and shoved each other, dodging each other's loads, and nearly knocked the maestro over.

If those brutes only knew who this man was they were pushing, they would treat him with more respect! And this despite the fact that our joy at reaching Cuba had given us rose-coloured spectacles. Everywhere there were signs of the aversion between Cubans and Spaniards, and we heard stories of battles as we passed.

'On the twenty-third, Lieutenant Barrios of the Cienfuegos garrison with twenty-five men from the Canaries battalion and eight civil guards fought a band of twenty rebels in Trujillo, killing two of them. They continued on to Palmira with the two bodies and five horses captured from the enemy.'

AFTER PASSING SEVERAL QUAYS crammed with whites, blacks Chinese, and mulattos, they went in search of a hostel. Itinerant vendors peddled their wares: sausages, *churros,* spicy and non-spicy *tamales.* On the pavements walked a multicoloured throng, women gossiped and haggled. Life pulsated like the sun that suddenly pierced the clouds.

Chané stopped in his tracks beside a poster stuck on the wall. He read for a while then grumbled irritably:

'We've arrived at a bad time!'

'What does it say?'

He read it aloud:

EDICT

La Habana, 10th March 1895

Don Emilio Calleja e Isasi
Governor General of the Island of Cuba:

Certain ungrateful persons, driven by excessive ambition, with no honourable banner to raise, and supported by disaffected workers and even criminals, are calling for civil war – anathema to cultured peoples everywhere and the ruin of the richest countries – according to information received from the civil governors in the provinces.

I would be failing in the duties of my office if I did not try to impede such sinister intentions within the measures at my disposal. Therefore, in accordance with Clause 4 of Article 2 of the Royal Decree of 9th January 1878, heard in La Habana Board of Regional Authorities, I

ORDER AND COMMAND

Article one: Public Order Law of 23rd April, 1870, will be applied in the territory of this island.

Article two: The Civil, Military and Judicial authorities will proceed with the implementation of the orders contained in the said Law.

La Habana, 23rd February 1895
EMILIO CALLEJA

'What do those words mean: disaffected, sinister, clause, decree...?' asked Lolita, always so avid to learn.

'Decree is an order, disaffected is when you stop liking someone, clause is a hole that is made deliberately, and sinister is what here they call being on the Left.'

'Well, I've got myself in a right mess; I don't understand anything that's happening in Cuba.'

Didn't she want to be free? That desire coincided with the course of history. Events germinating over the years meant that, once she was in Cuba, in her new life she too would be immersed in the whirlwind of change.

They went up San Lázaro Street among waiters, shop assistants, and tailors, courting, curtseying, and complimenting girls leaning out of windows. Others, who favoured more immediate romance, went to the Paseo de Carlos III, the Calzada de la Infanta, to Capellanes or Retiro, where they rented girls to spend an afternoon of pleasure.

On the balcony of a dilapidated house they saw a sign written in red:

León National Hostel

Chané went up, intending to rent a room fitting for his future diva of *bel canto*, he said. But after seeing the narrow dark corridors inside the León Hostel, and looking into some of its foul-smelling attic rooms, he began to curse his friend Pondal, who had recommended the hovel.

Dragging our trunk, we arrived at a pension in the Prado, managed by Galicians. We left very discouraged, however, and set off for Vedado where a Frenchman married to a German women ran a hostel.

In those days, Vedado was on a bluff overlooking the city, where gulls hovered and grapes grew in the undergrowth. In the late afternoon, laurel doves appeared in the sky; from the north, in winter, came gaggles of Florida geese; and wild cats came out at night until dawn.

Kitchen smells came up through the damp clothes on the washing line.

They showed us a simple but austere room, with a wooden crucifix in
place of the usual horseshoe.

The sea bathed the rock at the entrance to the hostel. Fishermen,
both black and white, went out to fish. The only danger in that
out-of-the way place were the stray dogs. Descended from the
Cuban bloodhound that were transported there to protect the
plantations, they now wandered sad and dejected, looking for a
master to belong to.

'Come up. Come up, friends. You'll like it here. Tell Marcelina
we have two more guests! And help them bring up their bags.'

Chapter Eleven

THOSE SPRING DAYS in the Caribbean saw frequent downpours. Lolita would have found them tiresome had it not been for her indefatigable love of reading. She read the Galician newspaper *El Avisador Comercial* from cover to cover and found the contents alarming:

'The military commander of this city, Don Pío Rivas, returned today from three days of manoeuvres with a hundred men of the Prince's Battalion, of which he is temporary commander. Overtaken and defeated by the enemy's vanguard troops, he left a dead Ethiopian in their hands. A curious detail I must mention is that when the soldiers went to recover the body of the negro soldier, they had to fight tooth and nail with the turkey buzzards that, driven by hunger, had savaged the corpse's eyes and face. You can see from this that food is not abundant in those parts, and it would be good for the buzzards if their case caught the attention of our charitable North American neighbours so that some animal protection charity could send battleships with food. I will not go on because it will make the poor buzzards' mouths, I mean beaks, water.'

Buzzards, Ethiopians, battleships... What did this jargon mean? It was unknown in Galicia. Why did they have to kill black people? At this rate there would soon be no Galicians left alive! I asked Chané if Ethiopians were the inhabitants of an African country. What was a man so far from home doing with the Spanish troops?

'You're too young to bother your head with this mishmash.'

'What's a mishmash, Señor Chané?'

'Nothing. As soon as the rain eases off, I'll take you to see the city.'

SHE GRABBED WORDS ON THE WING so they would not escape, and learned them like a parrot. Apropos of parrots, a story about her Uncle Ulpiano came to mind. He had appeared in Lanzós one day with two natural sons: a brown fox called Moses, the only male of a litter that by some miracle was not drowned in a bag with the rest, hence his biblical name; and a blaspheming chatterbox of a parrot, who had caused him no end of trouble for calling civil guards stupid and priests Satan.

Don Ulpiano reprimanded him daily, and although he was pretty tenacious himself, he got nowhere with the parrot.

'You're in line for the firing squad, Severito' – the talkative parrot's name – 'You can shout those insults in Cuba, but not in Spain. You only get away with it because nobody understands your foreign accent. Otherwise, it would be a different kettle of fish.'

The bird tilted his crest, and with a voice like a peal of bells, implored in his arpeggio.

'Ulpianito, *chico*, don't kill me…'

The parrot's verbosity was the talk of the town. A wide range of clientele came from all corners of Terra Cha to witness the bird's verbal skills, and have a coffee and cognac in the tavern for good measure.

Stubborn and tenacious, Ulpiano also wanted to show off his fox's talents: that he could tend chickens like a sheepdog tends sheep. He was determined to do it. But once the fox saw the coop was full to bursting, he dispatched them one by one to the stockpot. At the sight of the massacre, the last broiler bathed in blood and the devious fox covered in a cloud of feathers, the wretched Ulpiano, his eyes welling up with pitiful tears, uttered a phrase that would serve as a lesson for ever:

'Take care and watch your step. Friends in the coop, faith in foxes, law of the jungle!'

This caused me to reflect on the nature of uncontrolled freedom.

Chapter Twelve

'A DOG WHO DOESN'T WALK doesn't find a bone,' they told her at the pension. No sooner had she heard the phrase, she noted it down and wanted to put it straight into practice. Chané did not want to let her go alone, even though he felt unwell because of the time change.

They went in a carriage. There were hundreds of them, all of the type known as the 'Victoria'. You could hail one in any street, at any time of day or night. Well equipped with a Spanish harness and a Cuban horse, they circulated at high speed.

Chané soon went off to rehearse his solfeggio and she got caught up in the crowds of strangers, sometimes dawdling in shops with all class of clientele, and listening attentively to their conversations. In this way, her experience grew and she picked up words always useful to know.

I felt like an intruder in an unfathomable country, and found Cuba's indifference to me frightening. To me Labana was like a doll's barometer. A city covered with awnings in the morning and uncovered in the late afternoon; its citizens dressed and undressed with the sun.

Chané was not always on hand to advise her, so it had to be she, and she alone, who took the big decisions in her life.

I took one step forward and one step back, sweating cobs at the thought of having no job and no trade. It was three days since my arrival in Labana and twenty-some since my flight from Lanzós. In all that time, I had no news of my family or Graciano. I didn't know if they were among the living, or the dead.

Because of the intense heat, at daybreak shopkeepers unfurled the coloured awnings that had lain dormant in a rusty tube during the stifling night. Between the screeching and humidity, they emerged to transform the streets into a multicoloured stage set and protect the crowd from the scorching heat until the sun went down.

She noticed the ethnic mix, from the darkest black to the olive-skinned mulatto, known as 'yellow pine' or 'pale-face'.

It was said of them: 'God made chocolate, God made milk, but what He didn't make was milk chocolate.' There were white people too, of course, and thousands of Chinese men, but you never saw a Chinese woman.

And the sea. The sea, the ever changing sea. Yes, I had seen it in La Coruña before I disappeared into the bowels of the steamer. But nothing I experienced on the mainland prepared me for the emotions and feelings, capable of breaking bonds, triggered by the thundering of the waves. Infinite and sweet-smelling, they crashed relentlessly against the reef.

The sound of the waves, their contagious roar, gave her strength. She was on the threshold of a new life. The new language served as a springboard for new ideas, and with them, new emotions. On the quayside, she heard other voices, a vocabulary she understood better with the passing days, not only the words but that voluptuous way of pronouncing them. At first, it had been hard for her to understand words she had known from childhood, but which in Cuba had another meaning and another resonance. Later, with the gusto with which she devoured the dictionary, she would learn others, attracted by the sounds of those she already knew: *piérides, hespérides, pífano, pifiar*, beautiful words with a shape, sound and music from another world, which her ear and memory tried hard, if not to absorb, at least to get her lips around.

With the novelty of new words came the indispensable discovery. An epiphany, as the priests used to say, a strange word that to Loliña sounded like a hollow ritual, a swindle, a Christmas present she never received.

I remember her at the end, discarded in her room like a piece of junk. We followed her ramblings, knowing she was senile, that she remembered only what she chose to, and who knows what she invented.

'Ay, children, children, what you need is a good epiphany!'

IT DAWNED ON LOLITA that it was time to stop her torrent of thoughts tumbling out. It did not take long to wipe her childhood from her memory, and begin to think Lanzós had never existed, and if it had, it was mercifully hidden from her among memories that disappear with the setting sun. No, no trace remained of a past with other feelings. She had believed in it, but saw things differently now. She had a sensation she would never forget. She knew something new was about to happen. A born rebel, her spirit was like those wobbly toys that always finish the right way up. No traces were left of kisses on her lips, caresses on her body, nor memories in her mind. Even though her debut had been so recent, her heart was free to fall in love again. Everything was attractive to a young girl and corresponded to her idea of progress. In La Habana, chamber pots were taken up and down the stairs, instead of having to fumble round the furniture at night in search of outhouses. In the mornings, milkmen delivered their wares by donkey, basket and pitcher, whereas she would have had to milk the cows. People spoke in wonderment of electric bulbs, which gave tiny shocks and light.

How beautiful it was at night. There is no more splendid a sight than the Alameda de Paula at that hour. Do you see heads during the day? Well, you can count more lights there when it is dark. From a distance, it is as if all the stars in the firmament had gathered and fallen to earth. With electric light, you can read newspapers, posters, letters, as if it were midday, while in Lanzós we were humbly defended from the darkness by two carbide lanterns.

Chapter Thirteen

THE RETREATS AND MILITARY BANDS in the Plaza de la Catedral, together with the theatre, cabarets and *zarzuelas*, augured well for her life in the colony's capital. She too was a wobbly doll and didn't want to lie down under the cross she bore. She loved the concerts and political quadrilles that accompanied the death throes of the last decades of the advanced, modern century, while Spain made the same mistakes, sending more and more soldiers to the slaughterhouse, as she discovered in the press:

'The Asturias battalion, which arrived on 19th September, aboard the steamship *León XIII*, disembarked last night at La Bajada quay. The General's Company of Guides under the command of Señor Muguerza lead the valiant battalion out by Obispo Road and was showered with flowers, palms, tobacco and cigars among deafening cheers and applause. This enhanced the bravery and martial bearing of the troops passing down Mercaderes Street and up along Muralla Street. The ovation was doubtless deserved but it was nonetheless surprising that it was so enthusiastic and patriotic. On disembarking, the Asturias battalion's Lieutenant-Colonel Moragas received a luxurious gift (from Señor Palacios' shop 'Andalucian Stallion') of a beautiful machete with an artistically carved blade in an English-leather scabbard.'

Uninterested in the Asturias battalion and the Andalucian Stallion, I began walking round the city, determined to fend for myself and discover what life here was all about. Someone I met on the boat had told me that in the Plaza del Polvorín I would find a Galician woman called Manuela Riveiro, who owned a fruit cart or some such. I think I walked for more than six hours, asking directions. I found the Cubans so hard to

*understand, my vocabulary was still very poor, despite Graciano's effort
to teach me. They say Cuban is not really talking, but sliding the fleshy
part of the tongue around the roof of the mouth. And sometimes I even
found it strange to hear myself polishing the language like the sun polished
mother-of-pearl shells and truth to tell, I couldn't believe it was me. What
was painfully clear, though, was when they saw me with my suitcase and
my clogs they shouted, 'There goes a Galician hayseed!' And on top of
the insults, they sang to a son rhythm:*

*From milk comes cheese
From cheese come little cheeses
And from big Spaniards
Come little Spaniards*

'Born in a stable, you'll always smell,' muttered Lolita. She was
walking around looking for work, not to amuse the Cubans.

I registered at the Galician Centre, that is, at the Benemérita, *or the*
Quinta, *as they say here, or the Residence, as we would say at home. In
those days, all Spaniards arriving in Cuba had to become a member of
the* Benemérita. *And there they taught me to answer the Cubans who
insulted us:*

In Finland they call a hole a Cri
In Portugal they call an arse an ollo
*So I deduce when you say arsehole
What you mean is a* Criollo

*I marked my shoes in case I got robbed, because I was warned Labana
has lots of thieves, and they are called* cacos.

She was given addresses and went into shops, taverns, hostels,
run by Galicians, enquiring about any suitable jobs.

*Employees of the Galician Centre told me that if I turned left I would
find a laundry which hired Galicians. The owner, a rich man called Farias,
took me on. He seemed a little too fond of me, however. Seeing how well*

I did the work and made friends with his dog, he wanted to find me a good bed. But before night fell, I decided to go and find a more modest bed, but a single one.

The men in La Habana wore straw hats and long sleeved shirts. They roasted in the sun, but that was the fashion.

On her wanderings, she stopped to look in the windows of the big jewellery store La Acacia, owned by the Cores brothers, rich Galicians who imported to Cuba 'the latest models from Paris, New York and Pontevedra'. Dazzled by the brilliance, she gazed and gazed at the display of gold watch chains, jewellery, cameos, and other precious artefacts.

Some ornate pendants of old platinum filigree caught her eye; they bore no resemblance to the heavy silver hoops inherited from our grandmothers that on feast days encircled the ears of girls of marriageable age in Vilarrube or Mourence. One by one, she counted twenty-seven diamantes dangling from the mount: a silversmith's miracle, an inaccessible and distant mirage.

'Do you want to see how lovely they look on you, my dear?'

So bedazzled was she by the shiny earrings, she did not realise the owner was watching her through a crack with no risk of being seen himself. His expression was lewd and salacious.

'My ears aren't pierced, and they don't need to be.'

The Galician jeweller, used to evaluating women, fancied that this jewel with the gentle lilt he recognised as his parents' tongue, this little blue-eyed girl, a true caprice of gemology, was a real señorita, not one of those who gave their bodies for a couple of trinkets. He was about to return to the task in hand with a solid bit of bartering, when Lolita challenged him:

'Have you no respect for me?' she said, trying to tame a tongue which ran away with her when she was angry.

The libidinous eyes of the jeweller shone with more mineral than all the precious stones in his window.

Lolita reminded him in a loud voice of the warning she had heard in the hostel:

'Promise, promise until you're in. Promises forgotten, after you're in.'

'For God's sake, girl! How can such vulgarity come from the mouth of a little angel like you?'

By the end of the day I was exhausted yet invincible (words the newspapers used when referring to our poor little Spanish soldiers) and more determined than ever to survive, integrate and learn.

SHE GRADUALLY LOST the salty smell immigrant girls had between their legs, as every day at dawn she adventured into the maelstrom of the Malecón in search of work. She had a hard time, because the possibilities of finding a decent place were few and far between.

Memory sometimes plays tricks. I had so many jobs I can barely remember them all. With a keen eye, and no need of teachers, I was very soon no longer an apprentice. I assimilated things in a trice out of necessity, but I always knew I would never get what others got just by holding out my hand. I bore it all with fortitude, my eyes firmly on the future. If there were no future, the present would be disgusting.

LIKE ALL GALICIANS she began working in the Café Saberellas: twelve hours a day for thirty pesos a week, plus food. The employees slept together topsy turvy in the back of the café, although she got a corner near the toilet because she was appealing.

In the early morning, employees had to clean the café's stone floor. Her first job was washing the entrance hall. As luck would have it, the primitive system of sloshing buckets of water over the floor had been abandoned, and replaced by a metal hose attached to a manual pump. The pump was wielded unwillingly by a negro boy who never stopped moaning: 'With God I sleep, with God I awake. Don't make me work hard, I'll surely break.'

A dribble coming out of the spout occupied the boy for quite some time, fascinated by the huge curved metal rod he manipulated as if he was peeing, the pee hitting the ground with a ping.

This snip of a job didn't last long. After eight days they proposed she work for free for a year in the back of a tavern, with the promise of eventually paying her ten pesos. She got up at five in the morning, still in her slippers, with no time even to wash; and went to bed at midnight weary from selling so much wine.

Before moving into textiles, she worked 'in flour', as Galicians from the baking trade called it. That is, she walked for many a month around the city streets delivering bread, exhausted from the weight of the basket on her head.

After that, I was asked to work for the bakery on commission. They gave me fifteen pesos and food. We took out three ovensfull a day and had to deliver them. If I managed sixty pounds of bread a day, I earned twenty pesos and for every forty pounds over that, they gave me another five.

By talking to Cubans in the street so much, she soon lost her grating R's, the oceanic violence of the Z's, and took on Graciano's badly assimilated rough J, unknown in Galician.

They laughed at us in Labana. Criollo *ladies said we ate like animals and even dared to sing:*

> *Who says that a chestnut*
> *Can be called a fruit?*
> *Only a bastard pure and plain*
> *Who has come from Spain*

This work gave the opportunity to visit grand houses. Bread and biscuits from her establishment were much appreciated in those neighbourhoods.

I had many jobs in Cuba, some of them quite daring. Like all young people, I had come with no experience, no idea of how to make money, and no notion of how to get rich in business. On the contrary, I offered myself as a young girl, knowing no one, with very different aspirations from those of most emigrants and soldiers of fortune, and little knowledge of what awaited me.

Chapter Fourteen

ONE MARCH DAY, at six in the morning, fetid rubbish and puddles decorate the streets of La Habana, very few passers-by are about, and even fewer balconies have young ladies to be admired. At that time of day, there is no one to see or be seen, but Lolita is already off on her round.

On one of my rounds, I passed a big house which looked like the Cultural Club in Lanzós, except that here they call the style 'colonial'. A scent of aloe mixed with incense wafted towards me. Birds warbled joyfully, their songs emitted from deep in their throats. Suddenly, in a sunlit room, I saw a young girl of about fourteen seated at the piano, dressed in snow-white cotton. Her face, brushed with the slightest, the very slightest, touch of colour, reflected all the purity of innocence. She was playing a piece in a style that eclipsed anything I had heard before, or even imagined, despite all my familiarity with Galician choirs and bagpipes.

Affected, cloying, kitsch, and prim, the piece delighted the audience gathered in the salon. In attendance was the host, his daughter – the pianist herself – and Madame Yvonne, a rather short woman with a round face, her serene eyes compensating for the perpetual motion of her mouth, the tip of her tongue always at the ready to moisten her lips, grimace, whistle, or imitate the birds. She was voluminous of breast, lacking in waist, imprisoned in a corset, which made breathing very difficult, but gave her on the other hand a delightful blush.

The B major chords picked out by the little girl's left hand reached Lolita loud and clear as she stood outside the railings. They were followed by a series of arpeggios from the right hand. The tune evoked a barcarole. Now she understood Maestro Chané and those who accompanied him to the opera.

Seduced by the music, she took up her position outside the house every day at the same time. Instead of diminishing, her feelings and emotions grew. Eventually, the owner of the house invited her in. Lolita met the pianist and the audience, and the family ended up adopting her. She was given a uniform, the job of looking after Francisquilla and other household tasks.

It was an old house with green tiles, overlooking the sea, with its broken line of frothy waves sparkling at times in the sun's rays. The hall was beautiful, with its majestic ceiling painted with garlands of flowers, and on the walls were paintings by Madrazo and etchings by Goupil. From the ceiling hung hammocks which gently rocked the finest names in the Cuban art and literary world.

The host was Don Mario García Kohly, whose face reflected disquieting glimmers of intelligence and recklessness. He was in his early fifties, a scion of one of the few families who in former times had comprised the island's aristocracy. On his father's side, his lineage went back to one of Colombus's companions. And before his birth, six more or less opulent generations had been born and expired on the island.

García Kohly had just lit a taper of Campeche wood with a flint. Carried away by the aroma and the soothing melodies, he began to dream he was in front of the St Mark's Basilica, rocked by the poles of a gondolier.

A robust man of medium height, with a sprightly moustache and wide forehead, in his youth he had worked in Mexico on *El Imparcial*, *El Mundo* and *El Continente Americano*, all newspapers supporting Cuban independence. He had also been involved in separatist activities, but had abandoned them after disagreements with Antonio Maceo. He claimed, and no one could prove the contrary, that he had spent time with José Martí and was heir to Martí's conspiratorial enterprises. By always sitting on the fence, he became one of the foremost figures of the Republican Party. He advocated autonomy for the island without breaking ties with Spain, and even less with the Yankees. When we meet him, he is about to be named councillor on La Habana City Council. He is standing with his hands clasped under his stomach, like a monk entwining his fingers in prayer; his sad face looks slightly effeminate because of his misty eyes and fleshy nose, like some exotic animal.

They were celebrating the return to the island of the violinist José White, celebrated composer of 'La Bella Cubana'. White kept crossing and uncrossing his legs and making strange faces as he explained out of the side of his mouth – the other side was occupied by a huge cigar – the way to blow the clarinet, flute, piccolo, trumpet and trombone, all instruments he could indeed play. He amused the company present with his triumphs and exploits in Paris, especially when trying to convince them that he counted George Enesco and Jacques Thibaud among his students.

Curros Enríquez – who came regularly to the gathering – was not there that day, but they talked about him and his literary achievements. In the condescending manner upper classes show to more-inferior beings, they said they would introduce him to Lolita since he was her compatriot.

'I already know him,' she said curtly. 'He's a friend of my patron Maestro Chané.' They looked at each other in amazement.

A white magnolia, pruned by expert hands, refreshed the visitors on the Sunday the gathering was being entertained by Maestro Serafín; pianist, vegetarian, ne'er-do-well, and perennially broke. He sported a drooping blond moustache, and hands as ivory as the piano keys. Expert in the art of love, he had great success with the ladies, whom he aroused with poems by Ovid. Of a generous nature, with prodigious crown jewels, and always lavish with his favours, he had taken advantage of his orchestra's tour of Cuba to settle down there. His hands were capable of incomparable virtuosity, and not only for interpreting classical pieces, which was natural, but also for the mulattas buzzing around the brothels of Sagua or Santiago.

I refrain from describing his behaviour further, because I have not the wit, and one needs to see him for oneself to form an idea and stop beating around the bush.

The more vulgar women requested songs from *La Cebolleta* which was all the rage in Spain, while the distinguished *Criollo* ladies asked that he delight them with Debussy's *Claire de Lune*.

'I only play music I write. I sit at the piano and open the pages of the day, or night. So I play, for instance, the dying moments of the wind in a wood, the shining of a lover's eyes in the fire, or the reflection of stars in water.'

He approached the table and passed his hand over the candelabra, as if caressing the flame.

'Lots of stars?' asked in fascination Doña Inés, whose tongue always followed her emotions, and whose pert round breasts were a temptation even for those most accustomed to controlling their feelings.

The musician smiled and stroked Doña Inés' hair, having had a predictable reaction...

'Serafín is a butterfly,' said the *Criollo* ladies in lace, seduced, unsettled, apprehensive of his music and the likelihood of adultery, as if the appearance of the pianist were indelibly stamped on their foreheads at birth. Galician girls called him a gigolo; Castilians, franker in their language, called him a whoremonger; the more educated called him a libertine. But all of them blushed when they heard their mothers gossiping that a certain Serafín had a penchant for orgies.

He, on the other hand, felt comfortable with those elegant young ladies. Born in Mallorca into a rich family, he had learned the sacred texts because his parents thought him pure and predisposed to the priesthood. He wanted to ascend the ranks of the clergy, but had been thrown out of the seminary for speeding up the Ave Maria.

'The others were still at "Blessed art Thou" and I was already at "Among Women".'

Lolita was now a presumptuous housemaid. She came, went and watched from behind a mosquito net of the finest gauze, to see that nobody broke a glass and that everybody had enough Sunday *churros* with chocolate served on a little onyx table.

Beside her, five men were engaged in a heated conversation, peppering it with foreign names, and allusions to the war, and even went as far as to compare rebel ambushes with surprise assaults on the largest social gathering.

'The Cuban swamps keep swallowing up Spanish recruits and money, with no end in sight to the bloodshed.'

'León XIII blesses the war, the bishops in Madrid sprinkle holy water on fresh regiments and the politicians insist on making speeches that bear no resemblance to reality because war is good business.'

A man in favour of Yankee intervention butted in. His well-trimmed beard with a middle parting, and his pince-nez glasses on a rather timid nose, seemed to smell stock market reports in the rhododendrons. He gave off a hint of something polished and financially elegant. He didn't like the Spanish and unleashed a torrent of nationalist phobia.

It seemed to me this man was pissing outside the pot, because I thought Cuban society was pro-European. They were contemptuous of North Americans, whom they found barbaric and culturally inferior. Their wines were French, German, Italian; the conserves Spanish and French; the biscuits English, and so on and so forth. The best cooks were trained in French cuisine, like Alberto Herraiz who we had tending our stove, or else students of other famous Paris-educated chefs.

'How can anyone who has seen New York skyscrapers respect colonial patios with their columns, tiles and wells. They are so antiquated and old-fashioned, progress has rendered them obsolete. This country's misfortune is to have been colonised by the Spaniards and not by the English, so clever and practical in their commercial dealings. You only have to look at the difference between former English colonies and Spanish ones. How true is the saying "whoever sucks first, walks first". In any case, better crumbs from the king's table than favours from the lord and live with the cocks. But it's not too late to correct the past and give this land of drunks and revellers to its legitimate owners who rightly claim their manifest destiny. Thank goodness that many people in La Habana have worked long and hard to make this happen. We will come out on top and pocket so many dollars we will never have to work again.'

Others had heard tell that entire regiments had been decimated; that not a single soldier of the Cisneros battalion had survived, that mountains of corpses carpeted the ground and a whole factory was needed to make wooden crosses. I felt a shiver down my spine and it seemed a dream to be standing here calmly in the salon: sad, but with my natural sadness. I promised myself I would do everything I could to prevent so much suffering.

'The first thing we have to do is rid the country of Spaniards and fill it with Yankees. Their mere presence here will solve the problem. There will be beers all round, and we may not even have to move to the north.'

The pianist's blood was boiling. He waited for them to stop waving the flag, reminded them of the Yankees' ingratitude, and above all, that they were quite openly helping the rebels.

'They'll have their own reasons,' said Doctor Cardoso.

The pianist's heart almost burst out of his breast cheering for Spain, as long as he did not have to applaud the king or the monarchy.

García Kohly ended with an inflammatory speech, although with too much coughing and clearing the throat, against decadence, the fruit of laxity and licentiousness; and against the deceitful Yankees who were building their colonial empire on the ruins of ours.

It was all about words and utopias. '*Delenda est New York*,' the host signed off with a flourish. He predicted the unimaginable, that Spain would win the war.

The situation was so dire that in October 1895 Madrid sent Marshall Blanco to Cuba with a secret mission to recognise the autonomy of the island; ignoring the fact that the conservative bourgeoisie favoured annexation to the United States.

This caused a certain amount of concern in both Americans and Cubans, and signs of hope reached the island. There was already open talk of the *mambis'* war against the Spanish government. Public opinion had divided into two groups: those who wanted to see the end of the colonial system, and those who feared the substitution of one form of colonialism by another.

The Yankee supporter, who had been quiet for some time, narrowed his steely eyes and said:

'Soon you will be free.'

'Why?' asked García Kohly's wife, without understanding the significance of the words.

'Because the American people wish it,' replied the aforementioned male without abandoning his air of superiority.

Lolita dozed off, far from this artificial world of intrigues.

Why do we sometimes, suddenly and without rhyme or reason, flee our own country and live another life, hundreds, thousands, of kilometres away? Why do we have to bear the burden of several existences?

'LOLIÑA, COME QUICKLY, Obdulia's waters have broken!'

Although her cousin Obdulia had been about to release the fruit of her relations with Don Gabriel for several hours, her father was making her finish her chores.

'Go on,' he ordered, 'tidy the straw in the loft while you can!'

In my country women scythe the maize or the corn, trample the gorse, lift saddles and loads of cabbages, even though they are pregnant or nursing babies. At the end of the day the men relax and women start new chores: look after children who have been alone in the house all day; make the supper, and finally start spinning until well into the night.

Her cousin began to feel the heat of the liquid in the middle of a potato field. They took her home in an ox cart.

I went to fetch the midwife. When we arrived, the baby's rear end was already showing, covered in hair, placenta and liquid. Obdulia was standing up, the way women give birth in Galicia. My sister helped her first, and then the midwife took over. She had to push the foetus in again and turn it round. There was blood everywhere. Go and get the priest, I was told. So much blood, manipulating sexual organs, and the mystery of life put me in a state of sublime exhilaration. I reached the priest's house, in this case also the father of the baby, who in a couple of years' time the newborn would call uncle.

For Galician peasant girls it is not important if their children have fathers or not. In other places, women do everything for their husbands; here they do it for themselves, and since the men leave the land or emigrate, the women take over the house. They do not need men; they prefer to be independent and bring up their children as their own. The day comes when they are alone, free, and consult nothing but the movements of their hearts, or if they wish, their caprices.

I knew charming men of the cloth, but none like Father Gabriel, the first village priest I remember. He prepared us for our first communion and he took our first confession. He was a simple, humble, rustic man. He loved children and his faith was very clear. We girls used to ask him for picture cards of saints and rosaries that he took out of knapsack-like pockets in his cassock. He scared us with gestures like a shepherd chastising his dogs:

'Always begging, always begging! You're like priests!'

He was as nervous as any normal man under those circumstances, but even if he had been the bishop, Loliña would have thrown herself into his arms, unbuttoned his cassock, ten, fifteen, twenty, who knows how many more buttonholes.

He covered me with kisses and caresses, one hand on my naked breasts and the other up my skirt. I kissed him too. It was then I learned that priests wear trousers under their cassocks. I had never imagined it. I always thought they wore underpants with everything dangling. With so much fumbling, in a moment so brief he could not contain himself, the happy presbyter and new father came without his creative juices entering my body.

Chapter Fifteen

SHE AWOKE FROM HER REVERIE to the sound of José White's music and curious verses by Juan Montalva, an original poet who drew his inspiration from the daggers wrenched from his own heart.

Threading her way between columns draped with bitter lemons, she refilled the guests' glasses, sheltering the dainty Limoges jugs under her pert breasts with the same care that as a child she had protected the eggs that hens left carelessly on the threshing floor.

The piano fascinated her: an orchestra inside a piece of furniture, out of which soared syncopated rhythms and melodies often by Ignacio Cervantes. This and what the little girl played was real music. Every day she would stand entranced, listening to 'Lake Como', the piece Francisquilla practised so repetitively. Despite knowing it by heart, it always moved her deeply. But just thinking such a thing made her feel she was betraying the bagpipes of her native Galicia!

In my village, I was the child who best imitated the sparrow and the greenfinch, but I never imagined songs could be as beautiful as these.

SO ENGROSSED WAS SHE in the music, she did not notice drops falling on her white skirt and stockings – no doubt inherited from a demoted servant – spreading like the petals of a camellia.

'Lolita, for God's sake, I don't want you bleeding to death in Cuba like all those Spanish soldiers,' said the host, who had been watching her from the very first day.

Without a second thought, García Kohly went out onto the porch and neatly gathered up the most delicate of spider's webs, with criss-crossed opaline filaments like Brussels lace.

'Follow me,' he said. Lolita daintily picked up her skirts, and followed him into the salon, where they were alone, in the solitude of lovers. 'Don't they cure cuts with cobwebs and sugar in your country?'

'No, señor, we use cigarette paper and spit.'

'Cobwebs bring good luck, and should be harvested. They stop wounds becoming infected,' he said as he searched her foot for a bite, or a cut, or something. He seemed obsessed. 'I knew a colonel in the first War of Independence, owner of a huge hacienda along the Cauto River in Oriente province, who never allowed his house servants to dust cobwebs.'

Crimson with shame and embarrassment, Lolita had to confess.

'I haven't cut myself, señor, I am indisposed.'

Don Mario's nostrils flared and his eyes shone, suspended as he was between amazement and disbelief, boldness and embarrassment. He raised his head and kept his eyes fixed on her for some time. She vacillated between yes and no, I want to but I can't; but never between should and should not. Her positive instincts won her over, and she fell into his arms, taking extreme care not to get gored by his waxed moustache.

To me it was an appointment with destiny, and I could not rebuff it. In that moment of abandon, I forgot everything: my position as a maid, the difference in age, the presence of his wife nearby. I offered my lips and received his passionate yet furtive kiss, because the arguments over the state of the country were echoing in our ears.

He cared nothing for the violent stream spurting from my loins, nor the consequences of the crimson blood. He thrust himself into that serendipitous abundant spring until he created waves of fluids that ebbed and flowed, as she crouched like a gentle little animal in her lair.

Lolita lowered her head. The movement unleashed another flood that spread over her already stained skirts, because in each of her hands my dear grandmother held a miracle and a mystery.

For me this was the start of a life of pleasure, only clouded by how far I was from Graciano, the man I most loved in this world, and by my sorrow when I recalled how anxious he must feel about me.

They returned to the salon: she radiant and determined; he serene and victorious, as always.

'It was nothing,' he said, arrogantly, on his return. 'Just a drop of blood.'

I watched the door, terrified that when the señora came in she would notice the state of confusion I was trying in vain to control. Terror and excitement stood face to face in the void of my soul.

THE DISCUSSION HAD DIED DOWN, waiting for the host to return and reignite it. Mario did a triumphant round of his guests then continued his argument.

'Cuba is a model for Hispanic America. Spain is offering us a government just when the rest of the continent is torn apart by disputes and civil wars. Exports flourish while the other countries show only moderate growth at best. The traditional land-owning elites have been joined by new businessmen who are investing their profits in sugar and modern technology, in contrast to other post-independence countries.'

'This is doubtless the positive side of what Your Honour calls the Cuban model. But, it also has a negative side. Many Spanish capitalists and bureaucrats make fortunes here and remit them back home. The Spanish government takes its own surplus profit from Cuba, and uses it in Spain to wage war on us.'

'That's right, being a successful colony also has a price.'

The last speaker had not even finished when the little black boy, Anacleto, came rushing in, together with a mulatta in slippers, to take away the tablecloths and glasses. The last people left in the salon, sparkling clean as if bewitched, were a negro maid who went by the name Monguita, and Lola. Before they left, Monguita said with obvious double meaning: 'In clandestinity lies no money, love or infinity.'

'Be careful, child,' she added, 'play with fire and you get burnt;

life is like a palm tree, you have know how to climb; if you with a lion will fight, you will succumb to his might.'

She had guessed. As well as being a cook in the house and creator of refrains, Monguita was well versed in Santería. *She taught me the virtues of syncretism, which I realised had much in common with my mother's beliefs.*

Monguita was about twenty-nine. She was tall, fat, gleaming, a beautiful colour black, as well as having good healthy teeth and an easy smile. She was always joyous. She cared for Lola as if she were her own daughter.

I slept in a little cot next to hers, and her smile was the last thing I saw before falling asleep and the first after I awoke at dawn. Forty-odd years have passed and I remember the scene as if it were yesterday. One day she woke with a high temperature. I had never heard of more than forty degrees, but by the look on her face she seemed very ill to me. The señora wanted to call a doctor, but Monguita preferred to go to her mother, a former slave, and her grandmother from Africa who knew many remedies. They would cure her in no time. They lived in the old part of Labana where there were no open spaces, nor sea breezes, or nights scented with pines and poplars, but she wanted to be in her home. It was a long journey from Vedado. The señora called the coachman to harness the horses and we accompanied her. We had to dress her because she was unconscious. When we arrived they laid her at the foot of a ceiba, *because you need the permission of this all powerful tree to live.*

'Like it or not, you have to abide by Iroko,' said her mother. The whole family made a ring round the tree and intoned African chants. They took her to the countryside and a week later she came back looking radiant.

DOMESTIC WORK WAS tantamount to slavery in those days. Wages were derisory. The average pay in a rich house was three cents for a maid, a gardener, a kitchen boy or an outside manservant. If they were good milk cows, wet nurses could earn up to ten cents, the same as a master cook.

It was true that my house paid the best wages, because there were places where girls got no more than two cents. In comfortably-off families, the servants worked from six in the morning until well into the night. My house was one of the few that gave us rest time at midday and at eight in the evening we were free. However, we still only got one day off every fortnight. If you wanted to sleep outside the house two or three nights a week, you had to justify it by having a husband.

But how well they ate in the Kohly household! Pork and everything. The list of dishes was longer than Leporello's list of Don Giovanni's mistresses.

THE WAR DOMINATED EVERYTHING. The Spanish army increased hatred and precipitated disaster. To stop the advance of the insurgent army, General Valeriano Weyler planned to build concentration camps in Pinar del Río where Antonio Maceo's forces were.

'The *Diario de la Marina* says the Captain General has ordered civilians to gather in the towns within eight days. Any man remaining outside will be considered an insurgent and be condemned to death as such.'

'General Weyler wants to prevent the insurgents getting supplies. The peasants will be considered their allies, willing or unwilling, if they allow them to prolong the war.'

'We can't sustain another ten- or twenty-year conflict.'

'The North American press is also against us. They are inflaming things by revealing that 400,000 peaceful Cubans have been interned.'

'General Martínez Campos refused to consider any such tactic.'

'Of course, you need balls and Weyler has them.'

'As well as being terribly harsh, the measures mean the peasants' houses and fields will be destroyed and burnt. The negroes will have no option but to join the rebels.'

Monguita explained to me how the negroes saw things. Her brother Pancho had refused to fight in the war and fled to Santo Domingo. She, with her mother and other two brothers, later embarked on 'El Mambi' to join him. Crowded together in the hold, they endured real suffering. Her elder brother, Eduardo, cared for the youngest as he was dying of smallpox. Her poor mother had to dig a hole with her bare hands and wrap him in a shroud of palm leaves.

'Weyler is decimating the population in the west of Cuba. The people are starving and being left to their own resources.'

'Apart from increasing hatred of Spain, the social consequences are terrible. Large numbers of the internees die, and the others are left traumatised, unfit for anything. Overcrowding changes the way people live; a considerable number of women prostitute themselves to feed their children or their parents, moral paradigms crumble and many families disintegrate. Fifty-two thousand people have died in La Habana alone.'

It was still a subject of conversation in our social gatherings, but the press only referred to the situation obliquely and partially. Censorship increased considerably under Weyler; he prohibited talk of things everyone knew because they spread by word of mouth.

'Doctor Miguel Delfín is trying to find food for four thousand eight hundred children registered in the dispensary at *Nuestra Señora de la Caridad*. We'll have to contribute, tighten our belts.'

'Yes, and how did the numbers increase so quickly?'

'That's what the newspapers say, but *El Fígaro*, *El País*, *El Diario de la Marina*, and *La Lucha* are giving money under the table for the dispensaries, and the authorities aren't objecting.'

'They're lighting one candle for God, and another for the Devil.'

'In Galicia, they say one is good and the other isn't bad. But which is which?'

AFTER HIS FIRST BLOODY INCURSION, García Kohly did not need haemoglobin to lavish his attention on my dear grandmother. Whenever his wife went shopping, he would rush to get his *droit de seigneur* in the kitchen, or wherever Lola happened to be, ready and diligent. Since the most taboo topic had occurred that first time, all channels were open for new adventures. Fair game was the scullery while she washed the dishes with her back to the door. Another welcoming place was the charming vegetable garden, among plantains and papaya – fruit she would pick in her spare time – although as a bed it was somewhat uncomfortable. More inviting was the marital bed, whose sheets and pillows the maidservant would lovingly iron and smooth for the hero of the motherland to arrive sword at the ready to occupy places previously conquered.

ONCE THE FIRST HEAT OF PASSION had died down, my unease slowly disappeared. Mario – that is what he insisted I call him – kept his promise to respect me and was only tender towards me when he knew we were alone. If he wanted to talk about feelings he would refer to other people, placing in my blood the seed of unexplored yearning, and on my lips the desire to express it on other lips. The only barrier between us was the problem of how to address each other: formally or informally. I wanted the informal. The formality he demanded was too distant for me. Yet whenever I ventured to use a diminutive in our most loving moments, he rebuked me sharply, insisting on the form of respect.

But all in all, as intimacy grew, their lovemaking became more sensual and imaginative. The unhealthy modesty of the early days was followed by the pagan cult of nudity her lover demanded. She was how she had been as a child, delighting in looking at her body. But her budding self-admiration was different now. Before it was the manifestation of sensuality in an awakening body; now it was pride in possessing the ultimate weapon that tied her man to her.

Luck was indeed smiling on her. She polished her manners with Don Mario, and learned much from the conversations she overheard on the veranda with so many important figures.

From time to time, my conscience was pricked by the idea that Graciano would come looking for me and I would have to abandon this placid existence.

BATTLE (FOR A GAME IT WAS NOT) COMMENCED between the bourgeoisie captained by the legitimate wife, and the insurgent Lola, her successor. In the middle, was Monguita (who might be Admiral Cervera), who tried to swim between two tides without wetting her uniform. The duel lasted several years until the attraction of adultery wore off. It is worth mentioning because at serious moments you cannot talk in euphemisms, that on such a month and day, several years in the future, Lola's period did not come. She had been inseminated: in the Galician countryside this bovine synonym was always applied to women.

In this state, and in a moment of terror, I perceived the world lucidly and dug deeper into the obstacles that had hindered me until then. I remembered my beloved Graciano with such fondness, but time and distance combined to cloud his image. How strange; sometimes I thought about him and only felt emotions, nothing physical. So, I realised I only imagined I loved him, and that imagining things becomes just a habit.

WHEN EVERYTHING WAS back in its rightful place after the usual kind of arrangement, and the salon was calm, Juan José Ares appeared. He was a Galician with a club foot, a squint in his left eye, a big greasy nose and a face pockmarked by smallpox. He served at table in the dining room, and always arrived at the end of the morning gathering. It fell to Monguita to play Aída, Carmen, or Floria Tosca for him. He would go and fetch her from the sewing room.

'Señora Monga, pray do me the favour of coming for a moment to sing Madame Butterfly. I could sing without you, but it's not the same.'

We encouraged his efforts to entrap Monguita into rehearsing with him, because it was a real spectacle to see that clumsy Galician, burning with the divine fire of art, with his feather duster and dishcloth, twirling around the black woman and singing in his tuneless voice 'Celeste Aída', or Tosca's and Cavaradossi's arias. He sang in Italian and neither he nor

Monguita ever understood a thing. He would say, for example; 'My caddy from Nebraska' instead of 'Mi cadeva fra le braccia'.

Some friends from the Galician Centre organised a benefit night for him in the Gris Cinema, to help him out. But the Centre's director, alarmed by endless artistic ineptitude, forbade him to sing. 'How come a tenor is not allowed to sing at his own benefit?' he asked. The director reminded him that he was not yet a tenor, only a future tenor, and that he would sing in the Gris or the Metropolitan all in good time. With the small amount of money collected at the event, he bought a dinner jacket and got some visiting cards printed:

Juan José Ares. Future tenor

The cold of December and January had hotted up for Carnival. The coins had made holes in people's pockets and their carnival costumes were already worn. Big changes had been forecast for the turn of the century and for the terrible days ahead. However, thoughts of the century came and went much the same as saints' days and recipes do.

Chapter Sixteen

*AS THE YEAR 1898 DREW TO A CLOSE, García Kohly was
invited to* Las Delicias, *one of the most picturesque sugar mills in Cuba.
It was also known as the* Finca de los Monos, *because it was a kind of
castle-cum-zoo with about two hundred animals: gorillas, orangutans, and
other species equally terrifying to visitors. I was now part of the family, and
since Madame was indisposed, I went with Mario, his assistant Carrazos,
and a proud mulatto they called Chofur.*

Chofur got up into the front seat and clasped the steering wheel
of the first automobile in Cuba, a Mercedes from the French firm
La Parisienne. On the way out of La Habana, they passed well-
cultivated vegetable gardens. Peasant farmers emerged from huts
carrying primitive tools; sickles to cut grass and watering cans to
sprinkle earth from which squatting Chinese men in conical hats
seemed to sprout. They rattled along roads more suited to the ox
carts that had to get hastily out of the way to avoid being squashed
by the roadster racing by at fifteen kilometres an hour.

*That car seemed like a house with a bed in the back, a house that
snorted and shook. It was very high off the ground and had wheels like a
stout man with short legs. The horn, a spiral tube with a kind of rubber
pear at the end, barked 'Puawf-puawf-puawf!' It was so luxurious: an
astonishing sight for passers-by! We soon got used to the vertigo and
the fumes, but when we reached the plantation in the fertile plains of
Matanzas, the workers – all negroes, children of slaves – laughed at us as
we descended pale and nauseous after such intoxicating speed.*

'Don't be so insolent, filthy darkies! Hanging is too good for
you! You deserve to be minced and eaten for your own dinner,'
shouted the master, to show us how to treat freed slaves. But the
negroes had never seen anything like it and continued scrutinising

every centimetre of the carriage-car's four wheels and bodywork. They played *congas* on the horn – nearly tearing it off – and danced to the racket.

Before we left I had been told sugar plantations were kilometres and kilometres of sugar cane with large sheds in the middle where sugar came out. The foremen and workers bowed their heads as we passed by, and, sure enough, there in the middle of the undergrowth, was the sugar press. The plantation train ran to and fro, loaded with sugar cane for the smoke-engulfed monster to swallow.

THE NEGROES CLUNG TENACIOUSLY to their belief in the spirituality of the land. The same divinities live in the mountains and forests of Cuba as inhabit the African jungles. They are home to powerful spirits which negroes fear and venerate, just as they did in the days of the slave trade, and on whose benevolence or hostility depend success or failure in life.

On this translucent late afternoon, full of infinite promise, the negroes gathered in their barracoons to drown their sorrows with song and dance. They had finished their work day, hard labour from sun up to sun down, and were preparing food that they passed round raw, their palates apparently in no need of that unnecessary ceremony. The foreman appeared, whip in hand, to make them commence the dancing; the spectacle was already late.

THEY DANCED, AS THEY DID IN AFRICA, to express the life of their community, their religious ceremonies, tribal wars, harvests, and their erotic rituals because these natural people are much given to fornicating and enjoying themselves. They do not understand Christian worship and do not pray as we do. Whereas in Africa they dance to cure the sick and bury the dead, in Cuba they dance to transmit their cultural heritage to their descendents, to not forget their past, and to express their pain.

I enjoyed this diversion to which I was not accustomed. As the sun was setting, we wandered down the passageways, stopping at the main gate to watch the arms of the windmills turn. The blades of the crushing machines rotated as they churned the sugar, to finally emerge as straw-coloured powder.

The master of the plantation, a Catalan called Severa, was a friend of García Kohly. His word was law. He had guards, hired and paid by him, to make sure everyone at the mill was nice to visitors and obeyed his orders. Every night, all the negro labourers, young and old, men and women, took part in the music, some danced and others sang and clapped to the rhythm in the light of the moon, torches or candles.

> Blacks work a lot
> From below the waist
> But when they get married
> The work is not to their taste

A beatific expression illuminated the faces, but the innovations of the female dancers displeased the old men. An old Yoruba woman re-established order in the ceremony and came forward to greet them, addressing Lola.

'Señora, you have come to grace our country and ennoble our plantation. This sugar mill is your mill, this humble hut is your hut, and we are all your servants. By Ochún, do not deny us your favour or the pleasure of contemplating your beauty!' For which Lola thanked her amiably and gracefully.

THE DANCE SHE REMEMBERED MOST was the *Yuka*. There were three musicians each with a drum – the largest, the *caja*, then the *mula*, and the smallest, the *cachimba*. Behind them, two musicians tapped hollowed-out pieces of cedar wood. The dancers danced in pairs, shaking their bodies backwards and forwards, and jumping with their hands on their hips. Others sang to cheer on the jumpers, who made circles in the air like birds. In ritual language this meant that they were about to enter a state of ecstasy.

Although slavery had been abolished, the negroes were still, to all intents and purposes, slaves. The masters carried on the same, so did the foremen, who in the past had used machetes and pistols, and now egged them on with whips and dogs.

They did another dance for us, more complex and cruel, one they call maní. *They formed a ring of forty or fifty* maniseros. *They wore their work clothes, and round their heads and waists tied coloured patterned kerchiefs called* vayajú. *I don't know if it was a game or a pitched battle, because they gave each other a hell of a thrashing. For the* maní *blows to have greater effect, they also tied various fetishes round their wrists. Whoever's turn it was to be beaten, went out to dance. They shouted and yelled under the blows, and every now and again a huge negro would fall on someone who could not get up. The* maniseros *did not bet on the fights. I was told it happened at some sugar mills, I don't remember it being done at* Las Delicias. *But I do know the masters made sure the negroes didn't hurt each other too much, because sometimes their injuries meant they couldn't work for a week. The women did not fight, they just clapped in time to the music.*

The only complaint I had with the melodies was that they were too short. Each contained a very short phrase, repeated twenty or thirty times. Beautiful phrases no doubt but we were soon saturated, as you would be even with the most delicious of dishes. The negroes, on the other hand, seemed to take great delight in singing or listening to the same rhythm, as if they liked getting drunk on the same wine, whereas white people prefer to alternate their liquors.

At a sign from a priest – who seemed to be the genuine article – they all stood up and sang a chorus accompanied by a joyful rumba. When they had finished six women came forward to take their places.

Anyone who has seen a Spanish fandango, and then exaggerates the lewd gestures tenfold, will have some idea of the furious gesticulations these women were making. They seemed to want to demonstrate as much originality as they were allowed.

The six women were replaced by another six, and the dance went on for two more hours, until the drums were deafening. More and more women came forward, one by one, to dance their hearts out for an attentive audience that watched each movement with glazed eyes and murmurs of approval for their more than usually fascinating fondling.

The last dance began unhurriedly to a muscular rhythm led by a timbal. It signified the triumph of eroticism, the life cycle. With no false modesty or lewdness, but taking great pleasure in his skill, the dancer reflected the stages of the sexual act. Each roll of the drum was translated into movement: as the cadence quickened, so did his body; as the beat got louder, the higher he jumped. He danced the joy of anticipation, the anxiety of desire, then slowly, as the drum got excited, like blood pulsating in the veins, resurged the movements of frenetic passion, rapid, quick, man and drum in a symmetric violence. When the drum fell silent, the dancer collapsed exhausted. The whole dance lasted as long as the art of lovemaking; and as soon as one dancer fell to the floor, another replaced him and the act began over and over again through the night.

THE OLD YORUBA LADY who had greeted them, came up to Lola and said:

'Know that I see written on your forehead the many trials and tribulations you will face before discovering your true identity and becoming mistress of your fate. So, reward me for good news! I can tell you that you will have a double destiny, be the mother of a male child who will look after you in your old age, and you will die in the arms of your family.'

Remember that Lola was the daughter of a witch. She knew how to decipher magic petroglyphs and discover buried treasure, so she wasn't at all surprised by the predictions of the *santera*.

THE BEST PART CAME AT THE END. *At this plantation they would hold soirées where serious patriotic matters were also discussed. Ignacio Cervantes, and other songwriters, were often invited. Five negroes installed a grand piano in the middle of a circle, into which sprung a young* boy and a singer, also barely out of her teens. The master introduced them: his name was Eduardo Sánchez de Fuentes and she was Chalía Herrera.

Sánchez de Fuentes, some eighteen years old, was accompanying Chalía's rendering of an as yet unnamed composition.

Cubans: the heavens resound with
a voice that gives us strength
in the formidable struggle
the wise patriot undertook with glory

Overcome by the beauty of the song, I approached Eduardo to ask its title. He blushed, very nervously, and mumbled that he was waiting for inspiration to baptise it. He stammered... that in my honour... he stuttered... and withdrew to a corner with his brother Fernán, who had written the words. Shortly afterwards, he returned to the piano, to play the new version:

In Cuba,
Beautiful island of burning sun
Under its azure sky
Adorable brunette, of all the flowers
The queen is
You.

Sacred fire guards your heart
The clear sky
Gave you its joy
And in your gaze God confused
Your eyes for the night and the light
Of the sun's rays.

The palm tree, that in the wood gently
Lulled your dreams
And the breeze's kiss at dusk

Awakened you.
Cane is sweet, but more so your voice
That removes bitterness
From the heart.

And contemplating you
My lyre sighs
Blessing you, peerless beauty… ay!
Because Cuba is
You.

The soirée ended at four in the morning, when in the Caribbean the
night is at its darkest. I was very thrilled by the pianist's declaration.
Mario had been excited by the ritual dances. He told Carrazos he and I
would go back alone with the chauffeur, and made him stay at the sugar
mill for the night.

THE TEMPERATURE HAD DROPPED to fifteen degrees,
similar to Galicia, but Lola acclimatised slowly and she hadn't
thought of bringing a stole. The old Yoruba lady saw her goose
flesh and put a shawl around her shoulders. Lola had not been
wearing it long before she noticed a legion of fleas that made her
skin itch and she began scratching her head:

'Tell me, señora, why are there so many fleas in this shawl?'

'Take no notice, girl. They bother because you've just put it
on. After you wear it for a week, you'll forget the fleas and won't
feel a thing.'

Lola finally understood the deplorable state the negroes lived in,
and did not take the shawl off until the woman was out of sight.
Her head was spinning. García Kohly kept calling the chauffeur.

'Where are we going, señor?'

'Wherever you wish!'

He pushed Lola into the ready for bed Mercedes, and followed
her.

These combustion engine vehicles, almost all of them European makes, had just begun to arrive in Cuba in very small numbers, intended for discerning people. In the main, carriages were still the fashion. In the shade of the awnings on both sides of La Habana streets, passers-by could still hear the sound of horses' hoofs on the parquet pavements playing out their last quavers of a long history, plucked by the celestial ringing of the bells.

CHOFUR GAVE THE STARTING HANDLE *several turns and took up his position at the wheel. We set off at a phenomenal speed, terrified because not a single horse was pulling us. To demonstrate the power of the motor, Chofur headed for a river bank to climb a small hill that was barely a hill.*

'Turn towards Vedado,' ordered the masculine voice from the rear. The chauffeur obeyed somewhat peevishly – he would have preferred to go via Vibora, the road Kohly indicated being more uneven. Potholes, ruts, and bumps provoked jolting, rocking, and gasping from behind, and caused the excited eavesdropper to change down a few gears and take a look. The moon was in its fourteenth night and lit up the rear of the car.

'Go on, go on, step on it, don't stop,' urged that same voice.

'Where to?'

'Wherever you feel like, and slow down.'

They first skirted Linea, and after an hour, reached the Morro. The night grew darker and only the reflection of the moon on the sea tempered the deepening shadows.

The chauffer got down to give the starter handle a twirl. The engine sneezed and spluttered, and suddenly set off backwards, as if it didn't understand it was being asked to climb.

Mario and I began to shriek in unison: 'Stop, stop! Enough, please!' Chofur seized a crowbar and a tad embarrassed declared that we had to get down because the car couldn't climb with so much jostling going on in the back. We got down, wrapped in blankets, shaking with excitement and fear, and a mixture of respect and apprehension. Despite being empty, the car kept rolling backwards. We were worried, yes, but also amazed at the car's prowess, as enveloped in a cloud of black smoke, it finally teetered back uphill.

'You're a pile of shit, you shit mulatto,' bellowed Don Mario, not disturbed by the redundancy. The engine exhaled a few last gasps.

We encountered a herd of cows along Vedado. We peeped the horn and the cows approached us with curiosity. I waved my fan at them because I understood cows, and Don Mario shouted, 'Go away. Shoo!' They turned their backs on us to show they were unimpressed by progress.

The chauffeur kept up a running commentary about 'if the points this, or the crankshaft that, or the petrol or the overheating,' a whole orgy of new words that Lola retained in her subconscious. But the car reacted as the cows had: once its curiosity was satisfied, it lost interest. It stopped right there in the middle of the herd at the bottom of a slope and refused to budge. They arrived at seven in the morning, late and in a parlous state. All was silent, and a slight breeze refreshed the centre of La Habana. In the distance you could hear the vibrations of the little bells on the collars of the mules.

García Kohly swallowed a bitter pill en route. French literature had waxed lyrical about this type of shenanigans in the past. But no longer; things would not be the same again. In stagecoaches you could run the horses into the ground, but in cars you have to change gears if you don't want them to burn out.

I TOLD MONGUITA of the emotion I had felt as the negroes danced, and at Eduardo's blushes. 'Don't be surprised, pet. He fancied you, didn't he? In Cuba we're not as prudish as you are. Here we eat bread where we find it and flesh where we see it hanging.' As for the negro dances, she explained that they are representations of the act of coitus. They are exhortations to gods — Yemanyá and Ochún — who are like our gods but baptised differently. Monguita knew a lot about them, and invited me to watch a secret ceremony. I imagined she must be a priestess in one of these sects, at the very least.

Chapter Seventeen

THE SITUATION WAS BECOMING increasingly complex and difficult for Spain. The number of orphans in Pinar del Río rose to 1,700, and the colonial government faced the dilemma of either stopping the concentration of the population in the towns, or assuming its terrible consequences.

'In Villa Clara hunger has reached such proportions and smallpox is taking such a toll that to alleviate the situation, the military commander Antonio Jaime y Ramirez had to summon local ranchers and requisition their milk.'

'And the governor of Pinar del Río has just circulated a decree whereby local people must take in orphans and educate them.'

'By appealing to charity, the Spanish state is transferring the consequences of its own actions onto the shoulders of ordinary citizens, thereby minimising its responsibility.'

Weyler's tactic of concentration did not have the desired effect either. Insurgent bands roamed the outskirts of the city engaged in weapons smuggling. The most intransigent Spaniards, however, insisted the repression be continued, and the policy of starving the enemy into submission be tightened. So, while some thought concentration was ineffective, others lobbied to intensify it.

They gathered in a room near the kitchen. The flagstones on the floor showed signs of wear from five or six generations of skivvies, whose footsteps had left cavities where water collected after swilling.

A large table had always stood in the middle of the room and there were maps and bookshelves on the walls. There the four servants who Madame had chosen for education would meet. Like a punishment. Good works was the custom in this family. There was no clock, so to know what time lessons ended (no matter what the season), we would follow the movement of the shadows. After noon the sun traced a square of light on the floor which reflected the trees like moving lace. It meant the end of the torture.

TO ENTER THE LIBRARY, pantheon of silent books, she walked on tiptoe like a barn owl. The house was empty and Lola began reading out loud, imitating the inflections she heard in the street: 'The birds stopped singing. You couldn't hear the twittering of owls or other birds of bad portent.' One day, María Rosa, the local school teacher, heard her and advised her to not shut herself up with books, as she had read in various newspapers that a Spanish gentlemen had been driven mad by reading too much.

I did it to give the books a voice, and to convince them that they too could be heard. I didn't want them to suspect Madame Yvonne's curse had damned them so they couldn't reach us. One day Madame arrived with a new book. Enormous, and full of unfamiliar words, it was devilishly hard, especially since my mind was already struggling with difficult words: 'profusion, tooth powder, inconclusive, contracting party, orthopaedic corset.' But this book, for crying out loud, I didn't know a single one. All so strange, I even had trouble reading them: 'cha...pe... au, de...jeu...ner, fro...ma...ge'. How could the way we talked have changed so much by moving countries, in so short a time, and without me realising? My spirits sunk. Learning all that vocabulary and verbiage, at a rate of thirty words a day, it would take me at least a century to speak like a Cuban.

'Can't you see it says Paris, 1871? Too much lip and not enough brain!'

It turned out to be a French dictionary from some people called Bescherelle and Pons.

MADAME WAS NO FRIEND OF SCHOOLS where foreign ideas corrupted young people. She appointed Lola to teach reading, to cobble together the minimum needed to make the other servants presentable at social gatherings. But what usually happens in these countries is, no sooner does a person learn to read than they want to write. So, at the girls' request, she taught them joined-up writing for two consecutive hours, as if they were in infants' school.

It was agreed that the lady of the house would teach them Arithmetic and Geography, as well as Catechism and Religious History. After an initial hour with her, it was rare for one of the four not to come away with pinch marks on her body.

From the day the drops of blood fell, she vented her rage on me. She left my arms bloodied from so many scratches. In retrospect, I think she was suspicious of my happy laughter, my weary sighs, and because I would say to anyone who would listen that I really felt at home in Cuba.

Yvonne – have I said her name was Yvonne? – boasted she knew French. She received magazines via the French General Transatlantic Shipping and Postal Company, which sailed from Europe on the first and sixteenth of the month. She also read the *Album du bazaar parisien* and the *Courrier des dames*, where there were always snippets of news eulogising Don Mario.

She hid other books, magazines and even diaries that we were not allowed to see, not even over her shoulder. A couple, I remember, were the La Habana Telégrafo, *and the* Crónica de Cárdenas. *And if anyone dared touch those! Nor could we touch those other pages full of squiggles, which I soon learned were sung, not read.*

Yvonne was the most elegant woman in the capital. She stood out, with great confidence, among the assorted cashmeres, linens and cottons that were the fashion of the day. Dressmakers made her very low-cut dresses of soft wool, her breasts delicately veiled by diamonds or flimsy chiffon.

She understood French because she had been to Europe many times. And, thanks to my mimic's ear, it was not long before I learned by listening to her and the Haitians at voodoo rites. Sometimes she delighted me, especially when she sat in the back porch among the bitter lemons to smoke in secret. She rocked in the rocking chair as if she were not in Cuba, but on a transatlantic liner riding the waves in port. Then, God knows why,

98

those aquamarine eyes filled with tears and she murmured the same old drone of a ditty:

Adieu, Venise provençale,
Adieu, pays de mes amours.

AFTER REFRESHMENTS, the guests returned to their discussions, always the recurrent themes of politics and history. On the former, they trotted out information from newspapers, cartoons, and even magazines read in the Club library, or thumbed on the reading table of some charitable organisation. Much material was also gleaned from the dispatches and cuttings of foreign newspapers. They expounded their views by banging their fists, snorting with disdain, and brusque movements of the head, although García Kohly tried to impose a strict parliamentary blueprint, and reserved the right to concede the floor by rigorous sequence of preference.

THE SPRING OF NINETY-EIGHT was unpleasant and stormy, full of grudges and anxieties as a conflict with hazardous consequences approached. The alarm had sounded on the 15th of February when the battleship Maine was blown up in La Habana harbour, and immediate suspicion fell on the Spaniards.

Tactical arguments were offered in the Kohly social gathering by Dumas, Balaguer and Castelar.

'The battle of Santiago was a stupid mistake; a useful sacrifice. Cervera should have left those ships and made the sailors fight as infantrymen. Canons and infantry are what defend the city.'

'He received that stupid order, you know, the kind that politicians who know nothing about warfare give.'

'Any of those pen-pushers in Madrid should have known that if the squadron left Santiago Bay it would be bombarded, ship by ship. It was one of the cruellest episodes. It cuts me to the quick.'

'How admirable the courage of those Spanish sailors.'

'We honour them; we pay tribute to our heroes.'

'What do you know? Hold your tongue! Be off with you, troublemaker! How can you say that to me, my man, when I...? No, sir! Wrong, this is insane! You are mistaken.'

The arguments were confused, heated; Don Mario had to intervene.

'Come now, gentlemen. Leave it be. There is no reason for fisticuffs over so little.'

THEN CAME THE ANXIETY OF waiting for almost three months to see if the US government would declare war. Yankee banners were strung up all over the island, except on the Galician Centre. Against the advice of Eduardo Pondal and other illustrious friends, Curros Enríquez and Chané managed to get the Spanish flag flown. Although all three of them supported the rebels, their opinions differed: Pondal wanted to see Spanish colonialism defeated, while Curros and Chané cherished the hope that a Spanish victory would prevent Cuba falling into the hands of the new empire.

Chapter Eighteen

DESPITE THE BLOODTHIRSTY REGIME he imposed throughout the island, General Weyler was unable to prevent rioting in La Habana. He introduced a policy of generalised repression, hounding suspects and accusing them of 'collaborating' with the revolutionaries, and that included Spaniards with liberal tendencies. The activities of labour organisations were outlawed and some of their leaders deported.

It became dangerous for me to live in Labana. Egged on by Monguita, I took part in several strikes, and as a result I lost my job. I had to understand; García Kohly could not compromise his future through any imprudence on my part. My room was searched. The police confiscated my books and issued a warrant for my arrest. They accused me of aiding and abetting the revolution and distributing seditious literature. The arm of the law did not reach me, however, because Don Mario intervened on my behalf if I promised to go and live with Monguita in Regla, the negro quarter of Labana. Monguita agreed, proffering the saying, 'Absence is the best defence.' In Regla I would be protected and could devote myself fully to the negro movement. We set up house there, although we came back to work in the García Kohly mansion three times a week. At night and on holidays, I put all my energies into organising meetings.

THE EXPLOSION ON THE US BATTLESHIP MAINE, in La Habana harbour on 15th February, acted as a catalyst for the conflict. Avoiding war with the United States was now well nigh impossible, although public opinion had to be mobilised first. The Yankees took two months to prepare it. First to appear was a slogan designed to inflame anti-Spanish feeling and whip up the desire for war: 'Remember the *Maine*!' echoing 'Remember the

Alamo!' This vengeful battle-cry not only adorned newspaper headlines, but also appeared on pennants, lapel buttons, and even manufactured goods: clothes, shoes, necklaces, and other ornaments sporting the Stars and Stripes. Cartoons of the sinking of the *Maine* were published in the Montreal newspaper *Le Journal* and syndicated all over the US from the Atlantic to the Pacific. The *World* in Manila lampooned a bullfighter being given the *coup de grâce* by Uncle Sam.

Information was manipulated in Cuba too. The press published the obituaries of the victims of the explosion side by side on the same page as that of Lieutenant Colonel Joaquín Ruíz of the Royal Engineers, killed back on 13th December. His funeral was held on 19th February, and his body lain in state in the chapel of the Colón cemetery during the uproar over the sinking of the *Maine*, two days after its sailors were buried.

Life in Labana continued with seeming normality. People strolled in the parks, streets and avenues while hostilities ratcheted up. Someone painted over a picture decorating the wall of a tavern on the corner of Acosta and Inquisidor streets. It depicted one of our battleships firing at another which was sinking. Petitions lauding patriotic feeling appeared everywhere; one such was confectioned by La Colosal clothing store, proclaiming: 'Though we may all perish in the struggle, we must never accept the imposition of an ambitious and arrogant nation, that continually threatens us, and throws down the gauntlet to the weak government in Madrid.'

THE REPUBLIC WAS BORN, after a century-long incubation. The infant's first cries reflected a way of thinking that had been corrupted by the scepticism engendered by monarchies and privilege. The political birth of the Republic spawned hope, with the US occupation acting as midwife. Given the country's geographical position and rather small size, together with the moral and intellectual immaturity of its population, the idea of a free independent Cuba seemed wishful thinking. A tiny backward island twenty miles off the coast of the colossus that dominated the world could never become a nation with an identity of its own. The beautiful dream began to fade. Many honest men, like Enrique Varona, who fought for independence, lost their utopian vision; others less scrupulous gave this as a reason to indulge in personal enrichment. 'Well, what else can we do?' they asked. And to these were added the rest of the immoral scoundrels who needed no excuse to commit outrages.

ONE MORNING, on going out to put on the light on the veranda, Lola found there was no oil in the house and went to the grocer's. As she walked through the streets and squares, she noticed there were celebrations and merrymaking throughout the city. The shops, with garlands of flowers and eye-catching illuminations, competed to see who had dressed their windows with the most luxury and good taste.

It was as if the whole atmosphere had changed from one day to the next: parties, dances, firework displays, amorous trysts. The next morning at daybreak, when it was barely light, I went out to buy milk. The Galician shopkeeper had already adapted his shop sign to reflect the times. Arriving from Mugardos years ago, he named his shop '2nd of May', but when I arrived to make my purchases I saw an '0' had been added after the '2'. The sign now said '20th of May'.

THE PEOPLE GREETED the proclamation of the Republic joyfully. The election of Tomás Estrada Palma as President was practically a plebiscite. He was extremely popular, all the more so for being backed by the hero of the Independence War, General Máximo Gómez. Idolised by the whole country, his trajectory inspired the utmost confidence. Nevertheless, the fact that the Americans admired him made people slightly apprehensive.

Many of the Cubans exiled in Florida returned to celebrate Independence. The majority of them worked in the cigar-making industry, cradle of the trade union movement. No sooner had they stepped onto Cuban soil than they organised the Workers League, led by Enrique Messonier and Ramón

103

Rivero. We knew many agents from Washington had infiltrated the group. I acted as a go-between with the Spanish unions who were controlled by the anarchist movement. I went to their meetings and heard their arguments, which I can sum up by saying that the negroes' demands for preferential treatment served to divide the working class.

LITTLE BY LITTLE, peace affected even the closest relationships, engendering a feeling of mistrust. Some, like Señora García Kohly, thought the future could be guaranteed with words. One day she boasted to Monguita:

'*Negra*, I've joined the Country Club, you know.'

'And what is that?'

'Something you will never see even if you win first prize in the biggest raffle ever. The Club opened just last week. The building was designed by a French architect called Carpentier. I spent the day by the swimming pool.'

And Monguita, who was a *santera* and fortune-teller, replied:

'Ay, señora, there's a lot of water still to pass under the bridge. Who knows if one day I may be the one going to that Cuntri, and you won't have a place to lay your head.'

This thing about the Cuntri reminds me that as well as being prophetic, Monguita was the queen of irony. I remember once when Francisquilla came home after a week at boarding school, she told us how much she had enjoyed it.

'*We have a spiffing time at school, and on Sundays we go cycling…*'

'*You haven't asked after the Wonhu?*'

'*Who's the Wonhu, Monguita?*'

'*Your mother. The Wonhu who gave birth to you!*'

IT'S INDESCRIBABLE *the emotion I felt when going into a Chinese bazaar like the one Graciano opened for me in Lanzós. Labana is full of them, with exquisite wares from distant places. I loved buying Chinese things: pyjamas and slippers as well as crockery and statuettes of ivory and jade; I bought Francisquilla long stiff paper dolls, who stared with wide-open black eyes, and which weren't Chinese at all but Japanese; dainty kites – those true space travellers – and a profusion of fireworks, without which it was impossible to make enough din to celebrate the 20th May in those days. The Chinese also sold delicious tea and large* burato *handkerchiefs. We were all big tea drinkers, and we needed the hankies to tie round our throats when we had a cold, and to protect ourselves with real silk on* tronera *afternoons. The silk merchant could have brought all these wares to the house, of course, but we preferred to go out shopping.*

The illusion of Independence had turned job seeking on its head, especially finding posts in domestic service. Wealthy families left the country, including the few remaining doctors on the island. And those who could not leave at that time sent their children back to Spain alone, like sacks of potatoes. Rumour had it that President Estrada Palma had signed a contract to send youngsters to North America, and that the Yankees – who didn't believe in the saints or anything because they were materialists – put them to work in their camp in Guantánamo, where prisoners fried in the heat and all kinds of atrocities were done to them.

These had to be the offspring of well-to-do families because little negro kids were hanging around the street corners in our neighbourhood as usual, and even had a better time than ever because they paraded in the streets and got presents for Three Kings Day on 6th January.

AMONG THE TALL STORIES flying around in those days was the one saying there would be no more servants, which put all the madams in a tizzy because they wouldn't be able to do our work and didn't know what would become of them, so used were they to having everything done for them.

Some of them did not want to leave Cuba either and so began the fisticuffs over who would go first, whether the adults without the youngsters, or the children first and the parents afterwards, because they had to look after their old folks.

It was criminal to see those little ones boarding the boats alone (well, not quite alone, because they were accompanied by some priest or other, or some nun) and setting off for the unknown country of their parents, and I imagine it was even worse if it was true they were being sent to the North. But, to be honest, I didn't really give a fig either way. I had suffered enough by being separated from my family for so long, I'll never forget it. And anyway, there were so many other things to think about, such a kerfuffle right, left and centre, what with new ministers and officials, sabotage in the cane fields and proclamations against the independent government.

Chapter Nineteen

DESPITE THE FACT THAT the North Americans insisted the revolutionary army be disbanded and replaced by a legion of mercenaries, and the Platt Amendment be tacked on to the Cuban Constitution, the people welcomed the 20th May, 1902, with jubilation, as the beginning of the First Republic. The US government awarded itself the naval base at Guantánamo and the right to intervene in Cuban affairs whenever it wished, if it considered its interests were in danger. One intriguing paradox was that after three bitter years of war in the swamps – a kind of civil war – the Cubans and their governments allowed more than a million Spaniards, mostly Galicians, into Cuba between 1899 and 1923. This was obviously to the detriment of the negro population.

We breathed a sigh of relief when we saw the end of that wretched century, burying the last of our colonial dreams. The conflict wreaked havoc that still persists today. Curros Enríquez and my protector Chané were pretty long-faced and could not agree between themselves enough to compose the Galician anthem. We finally inaugurated it on the 20th December, 1907 at the Gran Teatro in Labana, but neither of them was the composer. The words were from a poem 'The Pines' by Eduardo Pondal and the music was by Pascual Veiga.

ONE DAY WHEN LOLA was happily out wandering the city streets, she heard a proclamation by the governor decreeing all shops be shut, and the population stay inside and not come out until order had been restored. The euphoria of victory had phases of looting, but the rebels put them down efficiently.

AMONG SPANIARDS, the end of the war, the defeat, produced certain worrying phenomena. They lost all sense of seasons, hours, years. That is, along with the loss of their own identity, they lost the notion of time. They did not know if they were old Spaniards, new Cubans, emerging *Criollos*, or obligatory Yankees. As guarantee or ultimate proof of an existence they felt was fading, or about to be erased, they wanted to show off personal adornments, particularly watches. Some began rummaging in old trunks for garments that had not had an airing since Velázquez was governor. They contemplated them with the joy of a child seeing a toy that is his, and his alone; or the wonder of savages spellbound by the glass beads they will receive in exchange for things of much more value to civilized man. Some put them on, wore them, and even went out in them. They swore they had nothing to wear and preferred this old-fashioned but elegant apparel, to the impersonal, worn and discoloured clothes of the new times. And so it was that people would come across images straight out of the Galician or Asturian countryside of yore right there in the street and, unable to believe their eyes, would pat themselves and examine their own clothes. They even began to imagine some inexplicable change had taken place overnight, and it would take half a century to understand what happened on that day, of that month, of that year, at those hours, minutes, seconds that the old clocks struck.

LABANA WAS A FEAST. Everyone was out in the street. There were just a few hoity-toities who would only go where the rich were, so the dust from the crowd did not sully their gaiters. The negroes celebrated the end of the war as if merely enjoying themselves would make them white. I was surprised at just how many of them there were, but I was told they had poured in from all over the country. Pure joy brought them onto the streets. Wherever you looked there was a negro. At first I thought they all looked alike, but after a few months I began to tell them apart, and each one looked different. Some were blacker than others: almost violet like the Mandinkas or yellowy like the Musongos. Now, of course, I can tell

*from a distance which nation they come from. The Congolese, for instance,
are short. There are tall Congolese, but it's not very common. The real
Congolese are short and squat. The females too. The Lucumís come in all
sizes. Some are more or less like the Mandinkas, who are the biggest. For
the life of me I don't understand this peculiarity. It is an incomprehensible
mystery, like the Trinity or arithmetic, but perhaps learned men can explain
it to me. Why some negroes are bigger than others?*

How could Lola understand if even the guests at high society
gatherings could not agree? For some, only whites born in Cuba
were Cubans. Negroes born on the island were not Cubans but
black *Criollos*, a different category altogether. For this dominant
social sector, the word Cuban, as well as meaning nationality,
clearly had a racist element to it.

Chapter Twenty

THE NAUSEA WAS increasingly frequent and impossible to ignore. The smell of washing soap made me feel sick, and so did scouring powder, which is supposed to be odourless.

She spent her time in the kitchen identifying the faintest of smells: the metallic secretion of tin and the viscous stench of sluggish cockroaches slipping between the cracks in the cupboards; the sharp reek of caustic soda coming off the floor; the whiff of small mice, light as tiny specks of dust. That is how she discovered the house's diminutive inhabitants, a *rebambaramba* of frightened creatures.

Aniseed liquor on the servants' breath, cigarette stubs rotting in corners: all these smells pierced the pit of my stomach like splinters until they made me retch. If I went out into the street to breathe, the stench of tar invaded all my pores.

AFTER INUMERABLE ERRANDS (getting advice from a *santera* and buying raffle tickets), Lola headed resolutely home, her blood boiling from some ruffian's cheek. She was always sent out to buy games of chance because, as Monguita said, the gods smiled on her: she was a medium and could bring luck. Scarcely had she crossed the threshold when Monguita, her hips undulating like boats, came out breathlessly to tell her:

'Go to him, child, without delay, apparently he's in a real paddy.'
'In a what?'
'In a tremendous strop.'
'A stupendous flop?'
'He's a real sourpuss today.'
For some time now, Mario had shown himself jealous,

authoritarian, and domineering. Poor Lola chose to stay absolutely silent in order to maintain their relationship.

She raced through the fresh dwindling daylight, disappearing down a passageway tiled like a draughtboard. The end of the corridor led to another floor. She climbed the dual stone staircase with its splendid bronze banister, stopping only to catch her breath, then continuing on to the floor above where Don Mario had his study. Her heart was thumping on arrival but she had lost none of her composure. She gave the bell the customary three rings, and García Kohly himself opened the door.

In his hand was a tortoiseshell pouch with a gold clasp; the size of a cigarette case. He held it out to the bewildered girl.

'And now, my girl, I'm going to tell you something I want you to think about each time you're purposefully evasive: if you make your bed, you lie on it; better be safe than sorry; don't bite off more than you can chew; and don't shit where you eat. Not once more. Understood?'

Lola was more hurt by the blackmailer's mellifluous hypocrisy than his flower histrionics. For a long time now she had found his ardour unpalatable, but this was the last straw. She said angrily:

'Don Mario, call me by my name, pray and don't be so familiar until you know who I really am.'

He banged the case down hard on the table. The earrings tinkled gently on their bed of velvet.

'And by the way, what does "purposefully" mean?' she asked Don Mario firmly, without the slightest hint of bitterness. 'And what's all that about making beds and lying on them?'

It would be another twenty years before she knew the answer and wore the earrings for the first time: the time it took for her to prove to herself she was more than just a maid.

Don Mario's moustache drooped, and he began to see her in a new light. He did not know how to regain her trust. He started taking her out, even in society.

The bond of affection was broken and proved impossible to

mend. At the end of one gathering at which libations flowed freely, Don Mario was overcome by emotion and began to cry like a baby, calling himself despicable in a loud voice, and even announcing he intended to leave his wife and children and marry this most saintly, most virtuous of women.

LOLA'S DUTIES ON CUBAN SOIL, scrupulously outlined by her master and lover, appeared to be those of a nun: dress Francisquilla, teach her to read, prepare her food, and look on with a bored expression while she played. A next door maid – co-opted into this service for a couple of *centavos* – even took the little girl to and from school. Lola's only pastimes were Mass and the circus, which the little girl adored.

The circus was the only spectacle permitted to young children. The Great Equestrian Company had been passed down from grandfathers to fathers, sons and grandsons. The artists all resembled each other: tall, powerfully built, and elegant in their well-cut evening dress – the kings of the ring. They brought the best acts from Cuba, Europe and 'foreign parts'. The audience dressed in all its finery for the shows, the focal point for the cream of society.

In those days, we were sated with all things African. At the table all talk was of wild animals, journeys to Africa, famous animal trainers. I fell in love, platonically you understand, with an English lion tamer who was performing that year. His name was Captain Wilson – all lion tamers were captains it seemed – and he actually died a month later in England, disembowelled by his African beasts. One day Francisquilla asked her father to buy her a lion. She was so vehement about it that he, with his usual method of never learning from other people's mistakes, asked if the circus would sell him a lion cub. It would not be a problem, but only at the end of the season. We made preparations in a greenhouse, where Madame Yvonne cultivated her palms and orchids. The animal would be better off in that cool dwelling than on the savannah itself. We ordered ten litres of milk per day from the farmer. When we went to get the animal, however, it was no longer a cub and Francisquilla was so frightened she didn't want it.

Chapter Twenty-One

ONE NIGHT WHEN my master and mistress were at the theatre, several negroes, friends of Monguita, came to the house, and I made their acquaintance. Among them was a certain Evaristo Estenoz, and a certain Pedro Ivonet. There were others but I don't remember their names. Monguita introduced them to me and both embraced me and showered me with kisses. Two veritable characters.

Monguita was a committed activist. Even before her bitter time in prison, she had suffered the horrors of the concentration camps decreed by that wretched little butcher of La Habana. Her voice trembled as she described the scenes of misery and death she had witnessed when Weyler rounded up the starving peasantry and concentrated them in the cities. At the gates of Camagüey, she had seen dead mothers with their babies hanging from their breasts.

Negroes were still considered no more than workhorses even though they had played a decisive role in the Independence War. In those early days of the Republic, they were seen, even by a goodly number of liberals, as a potentially dangerous ethnic group. In fact, they were denied full access to public life and had to organise themselves into the Independent Association of Colour.

The year 1908 emerges from the mists of time as a high point that neither time itself nor subsequent events will erase. The memories of my childhood coalesce, and I know for sure my life is marked by incidents I witnessed or lived through in my astonishing adolescence. But the definitive change took place in Amargura Street in Labana. Well it deserved its bitter name and I remember it as if it were yesterday. Monguita took me there, it was the house of Evaristo Estenoz, general of the Liberation Army. He had just founded the Independent Party of Colour. Monguita gave me its newspaper Previsión, *where Evaristo's speech was published.*

'The liberals are going around saying there's no such thing as a courageous negro or a sweet tamarind. "If ants were white, they would not be squashed" goes the popular refrain. But when a people are enraged, they do not mince their words. That is why we, without hate or bitterness, are forming an association of coloured people, outside the political parties, and we will force the authorities to sit up and take notice of us. None of the political parties have done anything concrete for us, no matter what promises they may have given. The truth is, negroes have no allies, nor do others want to be allied with us. Freedom is not requested; freedom is not begged; freedom is won. Rights are fought for and exercised. The danger we negroes see, is that the political parties will do their utmost to get us to join them, only to use us as unwitting tools in their own political machinations.'

The speech continued in what seemed like a breathless, lacklustre voice which from afar seemed to tail off inaudibly. But close to, it was like being led by the hand through a forest of parasites and lianas.

'But that discourse is a dead duck, a jester in the guise of a king, since the democracy the North Americans have handed us will be bogus as long as it ignores the aspirations of coloured people.'

THE INDEPENDENT ASSOCIATION OF COLOUR was made up of negro and mulatto war veterans. They denounced the new makeup of the independent army – all white – and the contempt with which negroes in public office were treated. And the same happened to those still fighting. When negroes surrendered on promises of clemency, they were killed in cold blood. Sometimes they were hacked to death by their own former officers, including negroes, who had offered their services to fight the rebels. Some of these then faced military tribunals and were condemned for their crimes. But the sentences were soon reduced and none of those convicted spent more than three months in jail.

Negro activists also fought the wave of Spanish immigration that they considered a deliberate prejudicial policy to Hispanise Cuban society. The fact was that while the War of Independence and US intervention brought about the political separation of Cuba from Spain, at the same time private Spanish companies were doing better than ever under the new Republic. The Hispano-Cuban Cultural Society was founded, Galicians played the main parts in popular theatre, and Spanish anarchists dominated the labour movement, especially the tobacco workers' union. Meanwhile, because they did not know how blacks were treated in the US, the majority of negroes appropriated a North American song, a refrain of which was repeated over and over again:

'*Advance, Lincoln, advance*
You are our hope'

Completely absorbed in her new life, losing all notion of time or the people around her, Lola learned like an automaton, always deep in discussion, and writing shorter and shorter letters to Graciano. She went to Mass every day with her charge, where she made new friends, and wrote pages and pages on everything that was going on in her head.

The cathedral was nearby. The first time I went, I was astonished to see rich people separated from the poor. The ladies went with their maidservants who would bring stools for their mistresses to sit on. The García Kohly family had a pew reserved. They let me sit beside the little girl, because they said I was her governess.

Chapter Twenty-Two

'STOP BROODING, GRACIANO. Clavixas told you she is very well placed in the household of a potentate who treats her with great affection; she already sings and writes very well.'

'Poor little thing. She's just a slip of a girl. She doesn't know anything about the world and they can spoil her for me.'

'She must have earned the wherewithal to return by now. Be patient for a few more years.'

'They'll seem like centuries. Time disappears faster for me than for her. So does money. I've already sold all my worldly goods. All I have left to redeem is the school.'

'Don't do it, Graciano. Not that. It isn't yours. It was your gift to Lanzós. What you give, you can't take away.'

'But they can take away my life, can they?'

Chapter Twenty-Three

ENVELOPED IN AN IMPERCEPTIBLE HAZE comes the memory of her first journey overseas; away from Cuba, that is. She examines her mind and finds no trace of a boat or anything; only now and then the mist clears and a chimney with a log fire and lots of snow appears.

We went to the United States, Evaristo and I, with Rafael Serra, to see if what was said about the situation of the blacks there was true. The first thing we did was to go to Fifth Avenue, where Carolina Otera was making her debut. The Galician singer with the face of the Virgin was having a liaison with Alfonso XII: her flashing eyes seduced the public more than her singing and dancing and provoked scandals with Vanderbilt and Joseph Kennedy. We were out of luck. As soon as she came on stage someone from the audience got up and shouted 'Hello, Cordeirana'. *She fled the theatre, leaving us all in the lurch. Afterwards I learned that she was angry because a cobbler from the village of Cordeira raped her when she was a little girl.*

Talking with black leaders, it seemed to us that although the social situation was worse than ours (it was a period of extreme racism, an average of three blacks were killed every week, either hanged, burnt alive or hacked to pieces), they were better organised and received more recognition from the federal government.

They thought the Cuban insurrection against Spain had been conceived as a movement for annexation, and some of the Cubans in Washington did indeed favour annexation. They had been talking about a revolution that would justify North American intervention for quite some time. These rumours were based on statements made to the New York Times *by a Cuban businessman, the head of Ceballos & Company: 'If the Cuban President sees that his government is unable to control the situation, he*

117

will ask the United States for help. This will mean first pacification, and then annexation.'

On her return to Cuba, Lola found that a whole shoal of sharks had emerged from within the Occupied Republic and hastened to play their part on stage in the national farce. In the shadow of the Yankees, they were rehearsing in their white drill suits, panama hats, canes with metal tips and diamantes on their little fingers. After the austerity and administrative honesty of the first Republican Government, the Cubans had learned from their North American masters the art of governing badly and getting rich in public positions.

THE TENACITY OF CURROS ENRÍQUEZ had managed to gather the various Galician choirs in La Habana into one choral society: the *Hércules* and the *Glorias* were combined as the *Ecos de Galicia*. When Chané returned from Galicia, they appointed him director of the new choir, so Lola had hardly seen him. Now in her very limited free time, she took singing classes. She had no notion of music and voices, but apparently had a soaring contralto *tessitura*.

We gave our debut performance in the Payret Theatre with Curros's poems set to music by Chané, highlighting the arrangements of 'Una noite na eira do trigo', 'Tangaraño', 'Un adiós a Mariquiña' and 'Os teus ollos.' Since I was the only one who could read, on one occasion they asked me to recite a poem Curros had composed for Chané.

'GRACIANO, STOP DRINKING, I SAY.'

'Come, my friend, I'll pay them with what they've taken from me.'

'Send news. I'll miss you.'

'You'll miss me? Let's drink to that. Come on, I'll buy you an *oruxo*.'

'All right, one last one.'

THE LANDSCAPE SURROUNDING ME permeated my skin.
I remember a daybreak and a sunset in Varadero: the full moon came up
from behind a pine tree, and the wave broke on the mango groves; the rain
bounced on the gravel, forming hollows in the earth, and gushing down
the cliff along gullies that opened between the rocks.

Varadero has a majestic beach. The families used to swim in front of their houses, which stood alone or in small groups some distance from each other. Very few bathers went from La Habana, only people with a house there. On the beach the girls formed circles of their own, the boys content to guess their hidden beauty from afar. And how hard their imaginations had to work to conjure up the divine shapes under that black alpaca garment with a white pinafore, which constituted the most daring bathing suit of the day!

LOLA TRAVELLED THE LENGTH AND BREADTH of the island, holding meetings with Evaristo, at which they told audiences of the conclusions they had reached on their journey to the North. She was the only white woman, and foreign at that, to accompany the Independent Party of Colour. But no one could deny Evaristo anything, and besides they took many precautions. Nonetheless she took her companion to task. She hoped their relationship would be transparent, that they both, together, would rise to the category of superior beings able to construct bonds of love, generosity, and intelligence. That is, that their intimate lives would reflect the qualities Evaristo preached in public. She scolded him because he calculated the political advantage too much when analysing the facts; it was naive, although perhaps her obsession with telling him so may have been slightly Machiavellian. She knew that a man in politics cannot be spontaneous. On the other hand, she knew instinctively that the audience were drawn to her because of her plain talking, and this made Evaristo jealous. He did not control her and so did not listen to her advice.

Chapter Twenty-Four

THE DISMAL DECEMBER MORNING dawned rainy and sad. Water drizzled from the sky without becoming an out-and-out downpour. It was not cold, rather a dampness that pierced the marrow.

Sadness, unease mixed with timorous hope, accompanied Graciano as he disembarked from the *Marqués de Comillas*. No one was waiting for him, he had told no one of his arrival. Despite his age, he had to run the gauntlet of the police, hygiene and even morality controls that all immigrants – men, women, and children – had to negotiate. But these proceedings did not displease him. His Loliña must have gone through them, and if he managed to follow her footsteps in this way, he could keep alive the hope of finding her, or even someone who could guide him to her door.

The doctors examined the immigrants' tongues only to see if they had money to part with. A certain René Cabrera had made a fortune providing certificates of good health to Chinese men for a couple of pesos. If not, they were sent to Tiscornia, where Galicians, Asians and Jews were all rounded up. There they waited until someone came to get them out.

Graciano went to Tiscornia in an open skiff. Seasickness, headache and the damp of the mist gave him a fever, aggravated by having to climb a hill. He soon realised the camp was surrounded by barbed wire, worse than a prison for an immigrant arriving ill and with no letter of recommendation.

They pushed him into a garden area with newly painted benches. Paradise. But it was closely followed by a pitch-black cell shared with a Japanese. They had cockroaches, bedbugs and fleas for neighbours, as well as guards who woke the residents at six in the morning with piercing whistles. The women were kept apart from the men to avoid contagious diseases and promiscuity.

With the first ray of light through a hole in the wall, the whistling redoubled. Kenji and he were summoned. Someone threw them a dishcloth and they had to wash with a hosepipe. The shock of the cold water told Graciano his fever was at scalding pitch. The cured him with quinine and *guaraná* syrup which tasted like poison. Kenji had his hair and beard cut; it was common knowledge they were treated better than Galicians.

Defecating on the ground – there were no toilets – gave Graciano a parasite called *Nertore Americano*. It lodged in his liver and made him walk like a man with porcelain balls.

The heat entered his pores. He sweated like a Catalan peddler, until he managed to change his corduroy jacket for a cotton shirt. The La Habana Galician Centre finally extricated him from there, advancing the regulatory sixty pesos.

Chapter Twenty-Five

IT WAS A FESTIVE TIME for the city. Nuestra Señora la Caridad del Cobre *had been proclaimed patron saint of Labana. Medallions and holy cards were on sale, with images of the Virgin Mary, the little boat with the black slave, and the two Indian brothers, who according to legend were about to sink when the Mother of God saved them on the high seas.*

A business in the city centre was exhibiting a huge sperm whale that had just died in the port. They had sprinkled it with formaldehyde and some other not very effective ingredients, so that a nauseous stench spread all over La Habana. As if that were not enough, on the other side of the plaza, some individual had put up a huge tent to exhibit mannequins with symptoms of syphilis. The figures demonstrated the horrors and purulence which venereal diseases can wreak on the human body. At the entrance stood a negro with a megaphone warning 'Roll up! Enter to a rumba and exit all defluted.'

GRACIANO'S FRIEND PONDAL suggested he could do worse than set up as a seller in the luxury textiles, trimmings and sequins market where young La Habana girls bought both for themselves and their madams. He accompanied him to see the person in charge of the stalls.

'It is our desire,' the poet declaimed, 'that you grant my dear brother the best-placed stall in the market, so he can sell his wares and take pleasure in the city and the nature of its inhabitants, and establish himself in all things concerning buying and selling.'

The *panjandrum* saw to it that he was given a stall in the very centre of the market; none were larger or more agreeable. And as well as being well-situated, it had a wooden counter that made it

122

comfortable too. The man then presented the keys to the Galician, by now dressed in his tradesman's outfit.

'Take them, and God willing, this stall will be a blessed place, and you will not have to go adventuring. Keep these bales of cloth and do trade with them: sell them at the highest price you can, the profit will be yours, I'll keep only the capital.'

Graciano set off immediately, going door to door with his bales on his shoulder, as tired and sweaty as a Catalan peddler: black Cubans, on seeing men in a worse state than themselves, would say, 'God, who wants to be white, if he had to be Catalan?' But he found no trace of Loliña. Finally, after following the most intricate of clues, he chose the most simple and straightforward one, picked from Edgar Allan Poe's 'Purloined Letter'.

After much going to and fro around the city streets, making enquiries in pensions, shops and bars, he spent two days asking questions in the offices and salons of the Galician Centre, until he heard the melody 'Dark Shadow' sung by female voices, and among them he intuited, discerned, recognised the timbre, tone, and *tessitura* of Loliña's voice when she sang in the parish choir in Lanzós. His heart almost stopped. It began thumping violently in his chest, but he dared not move an inch. After several minutes, he pulled himself together and entered the room. From afar he saw her, more of a woman, fuller of figure – with the passing of time she had become Dolores – but the same blue eyes, and gentle look, partly hidden by a Galician scarf on her head, led him to recognise the face of his Loliña.

He waited for her in the street. They came face to face. Without looking at him, or recognising him, she took the temperate path because it was time for her to go for a walk with Francisquilla.

From then on he watched out for her, followed her wherever she went, exhausted under bales from Sabadell and Tamburini. From daybreak he would stand at the railings of the García Kohly mansion to watch her coming and going around the house, increasingly dejected and decreasingly inclined to present himself.

Beside the front gate stood a polished pillar, and our man went over to leave his bundle there, thinking to rest a little and breathe in the aromas of the pleasant breeze wafting from the door of the house. He delighted in the pure and fragrant air. And suddenly his ears were caressed by a habanera played on piano, doubtless by pearly hands. He marvelled that such sublime sounds could exist and came back to listen to the concert several days running.

Those inside began to mutter, and became suspicious of the harmless, destitute tramp, smelling of alcohol and pestilence, marauding round the neighbourhood day and night. Don Mario decided to talk to him. The conversation turned nasty, degenerated into a fight, and finished with a challenge to a duel. In vain did Lola try to convince her lover it was beneath him to duel with a stranger.

'I do not even know what country he hails from; but let me tell you this, no other man would have dared overstep the mark and inflict such an offence. I am afraid news of it will spread and affect my reputation, especially from someone who is not of my blood or my standing.'

'Come, write him a letter, it may scare him off and he will desist in marauding.'

'In truth, I repeat, my dear, this peddler bears the mark of the devil himself. If not, how would he have dared employ such language, without fearing the ire of my sword? I could truly not avoid it, and it would not be just to hire a gunman to kill him. But if I let him live, his impudence will be boundless.'

Chapter Twenty-Six

ON ONE OCCASION, Lola had slipped out to the church nearby, just for a moment, no more. When she came home, she found the lock on the window broken and the little girl's wardrobe empty. Don Mario took advantage of the incident to reprimand her severely.

He brought up the matter after lunch one day. The slightest unfortunate incident will be inopportune for my career, he said after beating around the bush for some time.

'With the elections upon us,' he added, 'I have just founded the newspaper *Patria* with Méndez Capote. I have renounced my position as leader of the Republican majority, and hope to get a more important post in government. You are only six or seven weeks late.' He finally came to the crux of the matter. 'We still have time. Apparently it's easy nowadays. Hot baths, quinine, who knows exactly, we have to investigate.'

Don Mario obviously did not know. Suction abortion was not yet practised in Cuba in the early years of the twentieth century, although in other corners of the planet certain peoples had known of this method for hundreds, or even thousands of years. In any case, long before Dolores and Mario existed.

She had to agree to hot baths with gin, the effect of which was abundant sweating that left her face macerated but did not bring on her periods. She tried forced marches and running round the Víbora neighbourhood, as well as a lot of useless skipping.

'Look, Mario. If we have to have it, so be it. At the end of the day, it isn't such a drama. Don't be like that. Take it as a pause in your career.'

She wanted to smile at him, but he went off in a huff.

'It would be very bad for me at this particular time.'

He had been working on various bills which would establish him as the champion of moderate Liberalism and put him in the running for President of the Republic. On the one hand, he satisfied a goodly part of society that claimed new freedoms. On the other, with a clear conscience he gave the invader's capitalism a free hand to exploit the Cubans. Some of his proposals concerned the establishment of a mechanism for regulating or suppressing strikes, rules to govern the labour of women and children, the legalisation of divorce and even the codification of abortion, which he defended vehemently in meetings: 'The odd thing is that those who impose sterility on a large number of the female sex are alarmed at the spectre of birth control. I believe it would be more rational to evolve towards a system in which economic conditions and customs would allow every healthy able woman to have a limited number of children and raise them as effectively as possible.'

Chapter Twenty-Seven

NEWS OF THE DUEL spread quickly from street corner to street corner throughout the city. It caused a considerable surge of animated discussions in social gatherings, which always went on longer than usual in days prior to the encounter; not only because of interest in the result, but also because of conjecture over the techniques the adversaries would use – the Russian school, or the Italian. Old duelling treatises were dusted off in order to prove the efficiency of this or that sword thrust, and heated debates broke out among the members of the gatherings, who settled dialectical squabbles at the same time, as Alberto Fortes recounts. In a moment of heightened tension, a *pim pam pum* writer challenged another who was initiating his career as a critic with an article demolishing the work of the former. The inevitable happened. It came to the scribe's ears that the critic with well-founded proof had accused him, in his absence, of having plagiarised one of Maupassant's short stories. The prose writer slapped the critic with his glove, for the sake of honour and tradition only, you understand, with no wish for blood or wounds. But in the midst of all the kerfuffle, the copycat author began to take it unusually seriously and, courageously, the other responded in kind, so that each covered the other's chest with angry livid red marks, until one of the thrusts grazed the eye of the writer who had suffered the affront.

Certain scoundrels – known to everyone, but never sought by the police – introduced a horrible practice, commonly known as the lottery of death, which operated clandestinely. Its origin is hard to determine. Versions waver from accusing the government to blaming gangsters who, quite clearly, had infiltrated the ministries to such an extent there was no way of telling who was who. The truth is that betting games of all descriptions, like cock-fighting for example, have gone on in Cuba since time immemorial.

Equally morbid was the custom of betting on duels. There were all sorts of prizes: for who would win, after how many feints, victory by points, death or withdrawal. Many out-of-work Cubans lived off duelling. The fencing school potentates employed *mestizos* and likely lads, who for a pittance challenged old men who made amends in coin for the invented insolence, or put their life in danger by accepting the challenge.

The number of duels fought so shortly into the new century was startling. Every self-respecting man, every journalist whose integrity was called into question, every person who had any kind of public profile knew by heart the Code of Honour of Baron Athos de San Malato. The encounters were entertainment, they were the talk of the town, despite being prohibited, and villains sent their seconds on the slightest pretext. They might as well have announced it in the newspapers. The bouts usually took place in a field in the Bien Aparecida area of La Habana. Enthusiasm for this type of spectacle reached such a point that the main newspapers in the capital – *Diario de la Marina, La Discusión, El Mundo* – had a weapons room and their journalists were obliged by contract to take classes. What was called a 'personal matter' might befall them, for some skewed article or other they had written.

THE BARRACKS DOOR OPENED SUDDENLY. In the doorway stood a man with a youthful face and a direct gaze.

'Good afternoon. I am Maurizio Allegretti, fencing master. May I come in?'

'Please do,' mused García Kohly.

Don Mario was there with three or four officers. The Italian saluted.

'On Colonel Porrúa's orders, I've come to give you fencing lessons.'

As he said this, he took from under his arms two wooden swords and two blunt metal ones wrapped in several newspapers.

'When is the duel?'

'Sunday at six in the morning.'

'Oh, we have time. The day before yesterday I gave lessons to a young man only hours before his fight. Look here! I taught him an unstoppable sabre blow; but apparently, at the moment of truth, in a lapse of concentration, the stupid idiot raised his sword an inch too high, his adversary parried it, and left him face upwards on the ground, dead. I will teach you this blow, Señor Kohly, but pay attention, so that what happened to that unfortunate man does not happen to you. You will understand the need for precision.'

Dripping with sweat, García Kohly swallowed saliva.

'Can't you teach me the Lagardère thrust? It seems it is fatal…'

'My fencing art is simple and military, not as polished as the French. In Italy we learn little more than the counter-attack, the cut and the riposte.'

To demonstrate, Maurizio placed a human-sized mannequin in the middle of the room.

Ever since reading *The Three Musketeers*, the maestro had sported D'Artagnan's long hair, which he dyed blond to look even more like him.

'Here, take this!' And he threw one of the wooden swords to Kohly. '*En garde*!'

'I insist, it would be better if you taught me the Lagardère…'

'That is a century old. Besides, I don't use the foil,' the signore continued, as he swished the air elegantly with his blade. 'What I can teach you is the *metisaca* move that I learned from Fanto Fantini. The custom in duelling, at least in this city, is that you aim only to wound. But in a real fight or an assassination, the *metisaca* allows the rapid double hit: you wound once and withdraw the blade, and as the wound contracts, you hit again slightly to the right, and wound parallel to the first. The hit is right to left and down up. There is nothing better. Twenty years ago two detectives came to enquire if I had divulged it, because the woods were filling up with corpses. I was able to prove I had not taught anybody. My skill lies in that I see my opponent's neck very clearly and use the broad double-bladed sword. I go straight to the cut, not to point and slit, with half a spin like the executioner's axe. With sabres and modern flicks of the wrist, it is certain death.'

Don Mario, livid with rage, stammered:

'And... and... and what about the three... three musketeers?'

'Alexandre Dumas? Pouf... Good brand of cigars. But give me The Count of Monte Cristo any time.'

Apprentice bully García Kohly brandished the weapon like a robot, repeating the movements the maestro showed him with such stupidity that his face bore indelible signs of ineptitude.

'Quick, you wretch! Lightning on the attack, prudent in retreat, jumping tirelessly. *En garde!* Imitate my movements and keep yourself protected.'

Signore Allegretti raised his left arm with balletic grace and strutted confidently round the mannequin. He pulled it this way and that, positioning it to receive new attacks. In one of these he thrust at the neck, from right to left. The papier-mâché head hung by a thread on the chest before coming away altogether and fell to the floor where it lay, inert.

'Move the sabre to the left, Señor Kohly, so they can't split your liver in two unequal parts.'

García Kohly already saw his adversary in the role of animal hunter, his foot on the bloodied corpse of his prey. Those unfortunate verses of Berto Alfortes invaded his mind: 'I like to get up early to practise cut and thrust, I like to go to Cuban woods to bleed that pig Mario, I like the summertime to put my sabre up his arse.'

He shuddered. He had not slept a wink for a week, as if his death had already been announced in the press.

He figured that he was twenty kilos too heavy and many years too old to fight like Aramis. Panting, he told the maestro that firearms would put them on equal terms. His adversary was almost a quarter of a century older than himself and would be a bit too blind to aim straight.

'Very well, as you wish, things are hotting up,' said Allegretti suddenly. 'Do you think it matters to me that you get split in two? Are you a relative of mine? Do I actually know you? Do I know who you are? Am I not teaching you for you not to be dissected like a vulgar insect? It's for your own good, not mine!'

'THE DUEL, MY FRIENDS, if we don't want to end up in a boulevard farce,' interjected Colonel Tornamira, the *tessitura* of his voice drowning out the others, 'the duel has to be resolved in a serious manner. Do you think you can disembowel someone at fifty paces with a single bullet?'

This officer always made people feel uncomfortable. His nickname was 'Sword of Lucifer', and no man on earth was more stupid or more wretched, unless anyone knows anyone better at throwing a javelin, brandishing a sword, hoisting a lance or waging war with skill and cruelty.

He was, also, very ugly-looking: his face resembled a monkey and his presence was harder to bear than the absence of a friend. He wore the shadowy night and the venom of the infidel on his face like a sign of hell.

He was General Weyler's lieutenant, and had become famous, not only in the regiment but also in the division, for his bass voice, his enormous size, and his terrifying physical strength. The Butcher sent him from one company to another, and in under six months, due solely to the fear he instilled, he managed to turn the most anarchic and cowardly patrol into a machine that ran like clockwork.

'I tell you, and I repeat, that you read about duels of this kind every day in the French newspapers. The seconds go to the field, the duelists touch blades, and the newspapers write, "Fortunately, the duel ended without bloodshed. The adversaries fought bravely, but were not on target. They were reconciled after lunch with a hand shake."'

'Duels like that are stupid, gentlemen, and should be prohibited. They show cowardice and bring no justice to our society.'

Tornamira took the opportunity to rail against the feebleness and prudishness of modern times, source of all the misfortunes afflicting the island. And finishing off with an enigmatic phrase, he declared:

'Duels are principles.'

Señor García Kohly maintained an awkward silence. Everyone was ignoring him, but suddenly noticed his speechlessness. In the end, faced with the disproving eyes of the soldiers, he managed to stammer out:

'Well, gentlemen, I don't know, I may be wrong, but for me each case is unique, and has to be examined carefully. It's true a duel can be useful, and we all face it with composure. But also, sometimes, perhaps, the greater honour lies,' he added hypocritically, 'in forgiving. Of course, I don't know the circumstances of every case.'

No one was listening to him, and he looked anxiously at the officers one by one, searching for an approving face.

'Hey, listen, decadent politico, stop clowning about,' ordered Tornamira.

The candidate for the graveyard managed to catch the eye of Commander Palerm, who knew from experience how stifling this opprobrium is; sentences begun several times are left hanging, and out of shame you start again with different words.

'Allow me, Colonel. I will not speak for long. You said a duel at fifty paces with a single shot is a joke, and that only blood can wash away the offence. Then, Señor García Kohly wanted to tell us, more or less, if I understand him, he reminded us, I believe, of the words of the Gospel: "Turn the other cheek." Isn't that right? At least, that's what I learned in the seminary. He gave us his personal opinion, but due to the weight of fear on his shoulders and his deficient vocal chords – not a match for your operatic voice,

Colonel Tornamira – we could not hear his conclusion. In this respect, I want to tell you an anecdote that has nothing to do with our case but goes back, actually, to bygone days, to an American-style shoot-out between two officers. They bet their lives on the toss of a coin. But one of them, a very ingenious Pole, survivor of thousands of duels – it was not clear if he was called Wozzniak or Bosniaco – thought up an unbeatable trick: in cahoots with the judge, he stuck the tail sides of two coins together and while it was still spinning in the air he shouted "heads" and he was right.'

No sooner had Commander Palerm finished the story, than the penny dropped for García Kohly and he terminated the training session. One tour of the room and that was the end.

'Let's go and study the nature of the duel!'

YOUNG CUBANS AND *CRIOLLOS* went to the Prado to mingle with the Spanish among the Sunday spectators. Only the upper classes, some of them no longer young, women in phaetons, and certain scions of well-to-do families took an active part in the parade.

In the Prado there was a kind of carnival that the young girls used to their advantage. Their main activity consisted of recognising their friends, servants, saddlers among the masked revellers, and peeking over their half-open fans, greeting them in the impish and coquettish way typical of La Habana girls.

On those afternoons in Lent, though breakwaters scattered foam and the north wind cut to the marrow, the women wore low-cut dresses, their arms bare. Draped in velvet chiffon, they shivered under the beaver fur titbits tied delicately around their necks.

Each year that joyous fiesta, with its streamers, whistles and rattles, took on a new aspect and was of increasing interest to young visitors.

I no longer wanted to sit up with the coachman as used to be my passion. I now liked sitting in the carriage and instead of laughing out loud, rehearsed the smile of a young lady who knew she had a sensual mouth. For outings to the circus, Don Mario had given me a beautiful ermine muff, and we surreptitiously held hands in it so Francisquilla would not notice.

Chapter Twenty-Eight

AS SOON AS THE MORNING begins to break, the cloak of mist rises to reveal the feathery fronds of the palm trees. It is barely quarter past six on a spring day. While the hump-backed hills receive the Indians' first caress (that's what they call the sun in these parts), animals stretch their limbs and the peasants leave their huts to begin their daily toil.

The coachman driving García Kohly takes the Calzada del Carmelo. He stops on a plain, some distance from the city. The dew sits heavily on the leaves, giving the bushes a silvery hue. In the distance, like a huge barrier or ocean dike, appears a village, with its new dwellings, fir trees, and palms, rosy in the glow of the sun.

A few minutes after dawn, the cloud of mist fades and disperses, erased by the sun's rays, to reveal a number of black-clad men driving over the waste ground in an open carriage. The road ends, the seconds descend and disappear into a small wood.

Don Mario had begged me to come and observe, from a distance, a certain ceremony. I knew it involved a duel between my master and some unknown adversary, and it was as if I were indispensable to his victory. We walked until we came to a hollow thronged with very tall trees and such a leafy canopy no one could climb to the top. I hid as best I could among the foliage.

In the middle of the wood was a clearing that one might almost say was designed for the encounter. I sat on a log and, devoured by curiosity, watched to see where all this would end. I saw a pair of cranes descend on the breeze; brought there by fate no doubt, because they alighted on a net where they became trapped. They began to squawk and create a terrible hullabaloo. A hunter went and caught them; there was no redemption.

Then the adversaries arrived. They kneeled and kissed the earth between their hands.

García Kohly stays in the coach. Colonel Tornamira, in moustache and civilian clothes, goes in his place. He walks to the clearing with his seconds. The master of ceremonies reads the financial terms awaiting the winner:

'Know that if you are killed, the price of a free man is set out in the manual of Baron Athos of San Malato as one thousand *centenes*. But if you miss him, wound him, or cut him in any way, the price goes up to one thousand five hundred.'

From my hiding place, I could barely make them out. Through the vegetation, I saw not so much people, as grasshoppers ready to gobble each other up. My lover's adversary appeared to be an old man, unsteady on his feet, which meant he was the last to reach the spot where the others were waiting. Throwing their frock coats onto the grass, the two duellists stood face to face.

THE BRANCHES WAVE IN THE BREEZE. No bird or cricket song enlivens the air. Nature holds its tongue, humiliated by witnessing an impious act.

WHAT MEMORIES ARE THOSE that tortured me on an October afternoon thirty years ago? The hand that writes now only repeats what was already written, at a moment just like this, and persists on a grey and melancholy morning. With a long quill pen dipped in a porcelain inkwell, my hand is poised to fuse the two dates, 1908 and 1944. Both are confused in a present that will not return.

DON MARIO'S SECONDS take the pistols from a trunk. Then comes an incident, a moment of uncertainly that somehow humanises the ceremony. None of those present has ever taken part in a duel before and no one knows where or how the rivals must be placed or the witnesses must stand. Suddenly someone comes up with the solution.

'Gentlemen, we can do no better than turn to Chekhov, Lermontov or Turgenev, to find out how to stage a duel. They explain it often enough in their work.'

'Gravity, my dear seconds, let's be serious,' declared impatiently the man apparently officiating. 'We can't get those gentlemen out of bed at such an early hour. Let us begin by measuring the terrain.'

He takes three steps, as if to demonstrate how to count a metre. His assistant measures sixty, takes out his sword and marks the limits with it.

I felt a shiver run through my body when I saw the pistols. I imagined a head, an arm, a leg, covered in blood on the grass. I was tempted to run, and stand between them, to prevent the stupidity of their intentions. But I was an intruder there, so I remained immobile. The Code of Honour of some baron or other foresaw neither my presence nor my intervention. And despite watching so much of it, I could not fathom the full horror of it.

Before they give the signal, before his adversary is ready, Tornamira loads the pistol and raises it, coldly and calmly, up to eye level. No sooner has he raised it, in the blink of an eye, than his opponent falls to the ground, head before heels, and lies motionless at his second's feet.

As soon as he raised the gun, I saw the fire. Everyone ran towards the adversaries, shouting in desperation.

'Murderer! Murderer!'

Four more dull thuds were heard. That climate of violence was driving me insane. I held myself together by leaning against the tree. The dead man's chest was drenched in blood. Don Mario's seconds ran over to help him out of the carriage and congratulated him. The words reached me in my retreat.

'Bravo, bravo! You got him in one!'

Poor man, I said to myself, the other man. I left my hide-out, ran towards him, and found him laid out on a rush mat, his skin a ghoulish white, his death throes already passed. He was an old man, with several days of white stubble, and the corduroy trousers they wear in Galicia. I watched them take his shapeless red-stained bulk away, and put it on a stretcher which two men held out to receive him.

After the drama, I felt wretched and lonely. I could not get out of my head the poor victim they gathered up and took away like a bundle of rags to a place called a morgue. The next day I went to the mortuary to lay a wreath but the guards told me no corpses had been brought that day. Thinking back on it, I could have prayed for his soul, but it did not occur to me.

REPORT

To Your Honour the Government Representative in Cuba.

I have the honour to advise Your Honour that the duel between His Excellency Señor Don Mario García Kohly and a certain Graciano González took place this morning, 2nd June, in accordance with the pre-requisites submitted yesterday. The adversaries met at 6.10 am in the wood known as 'El Magüey' three and a half leagues from the city.

The duel, including the time required for the preparatory words of warning, lasted one minute and two seconds. On the order 'Forward', the two adversaries faced each other. The first shot from His Excellency Señor García Kohly hit the said Graciano in the upper right side of the stomach. His Excellency Señor García Kohly stopped firing and awaited his opponent's reply. When the required time for such a reply passed, and none came, it was established that the said Graciano was incapable of the act. Consequently, this individual's seconds declared their protegé unable to continue and asked that the duel be declared over. This was agreed amicably. During the journey to the hospital, His Excellency's adversary fell into a coma and after seven minutes succumbed to the consequences of an internal haemorrhage.

His Excellency Señor García Kohly's seconds were Señor Póveda del Moral, Captain General of garrison, and yours truly. Those of his adversary were the poet Enrique Curros and another Galician, musical director of a choir, who goes by the nickname of Chanel. By general agreement, I had been asked to officiate at the duel. I enclose a death certificate, signed by military doctor Cabrera Menor.

Captain Adjudant: Zoilo Valdesuso.

Chapter Twenty-Nine

I CONSOLED MYSELF with swashbuckling novels that Don Mario had bought to learn fencing, to no avail. Among them were The Duel *by Kuprin and short stories by Chekhov. From them I learned how to describe that fatal encounter, and realised that the act of taking up a pen alleviated my displeasure at the death. That is what led me to write, both as a way to learn, and to cope with life. I would write a short phrase, then find a similar one from the old masters to copy or compare. Hence I would put, 'I felt a glacial cold run through my body when they raised the pistols.' Then I would simplify a bit and it seemed more elegant. Also I put, 'My exalted fantasy made me see a head, an arm, a shuddering leg, covered in blood, on the fine dew-soaked grass.' I changed it, taking out adjectives and a gerund which I hate. I am also sensitive to cacophonies and consonances in reading. I have to erase a lot in order to write. I had started a sentence like this, 'It was the time of springtime,' with those two 'times', and after much thought, I put 'One day in spring', and then 'One spring day.'*

Given how good it makes me feel, since then I have written down as often as I can whatever passes through my head and my life, with no pretensions, and no objectives. However, I think I am at my best when inventing things. Nobody will be interested in my writings and I hope nobody ever sees them. I have them well hidden in the bottom of a trunk but will get them out when I'm old, to be able to go back and relive the life I found so beautiful. But I am far from being a Martí, a Curros Enríquez or a Pondal.

ABOUT FOUR YEARS after their first journey, they went back up to the North, and this time the memories are clear and precise.

We did not like it this time either, but this time it was because of the cold. We stayed in bed the whole day. We missed the freedom to come and go; we only went to indispensable meetings with representatives of the opposition. And how we missed white rice! From all the interviews, I realised that the way they represented the negro insurrection implied support for the sugar mills and the mining companies in Oriente province, most of which were in the hands of US companies. For instance, days after the insurrection began the stores of the Jaraguá Iron Company were ransacked. The owners of the company received help through the US consul in Santiago de Cuba, Mister Holaday, every time we initiated actions against them.

Chapter Thirty

'CHEER UP, DOLORES! Put calamities behin', the place is fine! Don't forget, I had to fool her by saying you're a young lady from Matanzas,' Monguita whispered in her ear as they climbed the stairs.

Sounds of weeping, shouting, and moaning descended from the floor above. That big old house was like a factory for restoring women's honour, with a vengeance; a labyrinth in which we had to find an empty room to fill with even more cries. We walked past miserable contrite faces to where, in the middle of the labyrinth, the stretcher awaited me.

A white-clad nurse comes to meet them, makes discreet signs for them to follow her, and takes them into an empty room. She must have grown used to the mysterious passage of so many anonymous women clients since her manner had acquired a reserve that typified the establishment.

The midwife, a woman of about twenty-five with a desirable body, is not long in coming.

She greeted me as if she had known me all her life. With luck I will never see her again, I told myself. This idea gave me much more courage than I imagined I had. She came towards me, obsequiously.

'Follow me.' And she opens the door of what could benevolently be called an operating theatre: a room with an oil fire and two beds.

'Everything is ready,' she adds to anyone within earshot.

I found the serious expression on her face disagreeable. She must have noticed I was looking at her somewhat mistrustfully, because she turned to me and stroked my chin like a mother.

'Don't be afraid, my child. What the doctor will do to you is less than nothing. It happens to the pure and impure alike.'

And then, to Monguita:

'We women are always victims. Men are like butterflies: they stop, leave their seeds and fly on. The consequences always fall on us. Nine months of aches and pains, the dangers of the actual birth, and then slavery: no more dances, diversions, parading; the wife stuck at home tending the baby and the husband out in the wider world chasing other skirts. Some of them, a tad negligent, trust in Apiolina pills, or purges with German schnapps, then come when they are five or six months gone, which is seriously imprudent. Others, very few, behave even worse. They wait until they are nearly due to say they don't want it, and ask us to rid them of the abominated baby, while the husband or lover insults the women, the midwife, everybody. Horrific: though fortunately the wretched unborn babies don't suffer on their way to limbo.'

I kept silent, captivated by the calm of the atmosphere that belied the horrors committed there. I almost forgot the shameful reason for my visit, seeing that they talked of everything except me, accepting my situation as the most natural thing in the world.

'How far gone is she?' asks a man in a white coat pointing his index finger at Lola's stomach. It turns out this is Doctor Carrión.

'About four weeks,' Monguita lies, dividing by almost half.

Doctor Carrión stops, consults the calendar he carries in his head, proffers an idea and gestures to her affectionately. It is obvious they have had previous encounters.

The small room we were in was charming and discreet, like the rest of the house: wicker furniture, oleographs, and painted plates on the walls. There were no windows to the outside. All the objects were bathed in a soft half-light which inspired confidence.

Two little knocks resounded on the partition.

'We're ready,' announces the midwife, 'the previous lady has left.' And she begs Monguita, 'Tell this young lady not to be afraid. After she sees what it is, she'll laugh at her fears.'

I saw the midwife get up and I began to tremble. I remained quietly in the armchair. Monguita offered me her arm to help me up.

'Come, girlie, don't be chicken. If you show you're afraid, even dogs pee on you. Just pray to mother Yemayá and you'll pull through.'

I let myself be led to another room, pinning my hopes on this compassionate doctor. There was an old white table covered in wine-coloured stains, and a metal cupboard containing flasks, instruments, and various foetuses swimming in glass jars. Several syringes, douches, and rubber cushions hanging from the walls completed the picture. The miserable trappings were not in keeping with the midwife.

'Is she wearing a corset?'

'No, she has come prepared,' replies Monguita.

They put a cushion on the table and made me lie on my back. Then they covered me with a sheet and rolled up my clothes to above my kidneys. I felt the cold of the rubber under my hips and shuddered. The midwife burst out laughing:

'What a scaredy-cat, cowardy custard! Quaking for such a tiny peccadillo!'

She placed my legs in the iron stirrups fixed to the table as she talked, like a ventriloquist.

'Are you comfortable? Aha! There, there, don't move. It's a simple douche. Is it too cold?'

I felt penetrated by the burst of irrigation which washed around my organs inside me.

'Come on, that's it. Now keep calm, all right?'

I saw the shiny broad speculum in the doctor's hands, and I flinched in terror.

'Keep your legs still! Don't close your knees. There, there... see?'

The oiled metal delved deep into me. I was immobilised by fear. I heard the noise of the instrument and felt my insides split in two. I squeezed Monguita's hand and dug my nails into her flesh.

'Come on, hold on,' she tells her, her hands holding the curls on her sweating forehead.

Bending over the lens, the doctor suddenly exclaims, unable to contain his surprise.

'Oh, what a neck, my child! It's a miracle anyone fertilised you.

We'll have a problem fixing the probe. Were your first periods painful?'

You would have needed the strength of a hundred mambís to bear what followed those words. With my flesh dilated by the metal, I heard the rasp of the instrument scraping viciously at the obstacle. Three, four times he tried to fix the probe and a couple of other times he had to pause, then start drilling and ripping again. I begged and moaned, held down by Monguita, who kept whispering in my ear:

'Be brave, be brave… a little more patience, it's nearly over. Repeat with me, "*Santa Yemayá de mij'amore…*"'

A wave of nausea swept over me, I knew I was going to faint. How long was I unconscious? I couldn't say. But at that very moment the other Dolores awoke with a clear, firm and unstoppable decision. My uterus suddenly hardened like a porcelain bowl full of tubes, probes, and cotton wool.

'Open up, for the sake of Ochún,' implores Monguita, changing her god. The midwife loses her temper and says impatiently 'We can't go on like this. You'll be leaving in the state you came in.'

I had always asked myself whether a woman who fights for a cause should form family bonds, since her personal destiny is to serve the cause and nothing should divert her from it. In the early days as an activist with the Independents of Colour, and afterwards when I started working with the anarchists, the answer was no. At this moment, however, I realised this was not true. A fighter, woman or man, has the same physical needs as any of their fellow human beings. They have to behave like normal people. What's more, in some aspects of life, it is their duty to behave in an exemplary fashion. Anyone who says they're fighting for a fairer and more humane society cannot practise the opposite either in public or in private.

Driven by that moral strength of purpose, she lashes out, overturning the bowl of boiling water, and scattering the cloths and soapy liquid. Pommels of disinfectant go flying through the air and splinter on the floor tiles. A smell of potions, ether, iodine, methyl and formaldehyde pervades the room.

Monguita begins picking up Dolores's clothes, to get her dressed after the aborted abortion. The midwife gathers the utensils and, just in case, recommends she rest a while before walking.

But she has not even time to survey the mess she is leaving. She rushes out of that decency restoring workshop with her plaits awry and breasts adrift; Monguita's heart sinking, and she gasping like a frightened bird.

I ran through the streets without seeing, or hearing. My head so throbbing with confusion I couldn't even breathe.

She arrives panting at her back door and throws herself face down in a yucca. It receives her into its verdant bed, and she falls asleep, exhausted. With her trail of curls spreading down her back and her clothes clinging to her body, she looks like a fallen angel. She is still a whole woman but urinates on herself from fear.

I was in a void, milky with sap, an airless pit, without bars. Even now the thought makes me nauseous. The same way the sea air does. Never again do I want to live in a sea port.

Chapter Thirty-One

IN THE DAYS THAT FOLLOWED, she kept pestering Monguita, trying to worm details out of her, reproaching her, or asking her point blank – even in front of the servants – if Don Mario had asked her to take any other servant girls to the doctor. Until one day the black woman sounded off, fed up with so much harassment:

'Stop playing dumb, my girl. The frying pan must get used to having its arse burnt. These people only want you for entertainment. Children? They already have plenty with their own. To you, Don Mario is so refined and polished, but he is a loose cannon. But he didn't ask me to take you. What does he care, he's a free-thinker, or some such. Haven't you seen the magazines he reads? It was Madame Yvonne. She doesn't want tongues wagging, and being made to look silly, and even less feeding other people's children, which is the most likely. Don Mario is always cheapening the family name by having affairs. And of course I've had to take quite a few to the abortion shop. What d'you expect? He spins them all the same yarn. What you have to do is keep working in our cause and find yourself a decent house, maybe with a French family in Santiago.'

It was a revelation. I suddenly realised what I was worth, and it was not much. I listed my assets: twenty-eight years old, a body oozing health, time in the future, and little else. I didn't even know how to bring up children, especially in the city. Back home, babies at a few days old were put in a basket and left on the threshing floor while their mothers worked. They survived as best they could, and those who couldn't went to be little angels in the sky. So I promised myself the one thing no one would take from me was words, that I could use them. I would make up lies, whole truths and half truths, just like everyone else.

She deduced that the way young ladies could get to be admirable writers was to see that words and ideas hung together like meat on the bone; and were in themselves a means of expressing all things good and all things evil. From now on, she would learn all the words and expressions she could, and write them down on scraps of wrapping paper.

Words of hearing, words of seeing, words of smelling, as they said them in Cuba, reflecting local customs, some with double meaning: dar candela (go mental), dar hielo (be frosty), chupar el rabo a la jutía (get legless), crica (pussy). The ones I had most trouble with were jicotea *(wasp),* tatagua *(moth, also form of witch),* chichinguaco *(some sort of smell),* guanajo *(turkey). I wrote them down and marinated them in a glass of honey like Monguita showed me, the idea being to sweeten words so they stayed in your head once you had learned them. The ones making their debut replaced the ones I had learned from my mother in Galicia —* lamigueiro, avelaiña, vagalume, aloumiños *their meaning faded in my memory and lost the effect they once had. How many had I left behind?*

THE CUBAN *CRIOLLO* BOURGEOISIE was less forgiving than the Galician peasantry. Don Mario watched his hopes of a brilliant career diminish as his maid's belly grew. Their relations had deteriorated since the failed abortion. Every now and again he made allusions to the need to put some distance between each other, without her grasping their meaning.

LOLA AND ESTENOZ had met again by chance at a ceremony in the cathedral. The Spanish army had invited important political figures to attend the exhumation of the remains of Christopher Columbus, which had lain there since 1795. This imperial act was the first in a series of events organised to return the bones to the Mother Country. Don Mario found himself 'unable to attend in person', as they say, so he sent his daughter, with Lola as chaperone.

There we were, the bishop, a historian, two forensic experts, Francisquilla, other important figures, and myself, breast uplifted by the national anthem.

The act of opening the caskets began. It was assumed that the first one, made of mahogany, would contain the remains of the Discoverer, and the second, made of nopal, a copy of the Constitution of the Spanish Crown with documents about the foundation of La Habana.

The idea of seeing the rotted corpse of such a famous Galician, as Pondal called him, was already an emotional moment. We watched the coffin out of the corner of our eyes. The lid was opened. Bewildered voices slowly petered out. Sopranos and notaries held their breath. Then, only silence, a couple of centimetres of earth, and some bones that looked like dogs' or cats'. Nothing else. Yes, some wooden wedges suggested someone had taken out another urn that had once been enclosed there.

The Mayor was lost for words; he continued the ceremony amid gestures and looks of amazement. When he had finished, the Dean picked up dust and bones to keep in the tabernacle of the main sacristy, all under military custody. The Cubans were relieved to see the suspicious ashes put on board a boat, bound for Europe.

Evaristo had been refused entry, and not only for being a negro. The fact is he had hundreds of followers hidden in the cloisters and the police discovered them. As I came out, I bumped into him and we renewed our friendship. He took me to the Gris Cinema; it was my first time. I came out terrified, truly. In the film, the main character was a convict, with a fearsome face and black-and-white-striped attire. My memory has not retained the details of the film. But what I will never forget is that the convict suddenly started to fall to pieces and the white stripes began to move away from the black ones. The Gris had a pianola and a presenter. The pianola repeated the interminable habaneras and waltzes. If the film was halfway romantic, it merited the 'The Blue Danube.' If it was jolly, 'The Merry Widow'. The presenter hid behind the pianola. He animated the film with monologues, dialogues and even polyphonic groups. Two or three times per session he emerged from anonymity and mounted the stage with a placard saying 'Five Minutes Interval to Prepare Part Two'. Sometimes the boy who brought the reels from the Vedado cinema, where they were showing the same film, was late, so the announcer entertained the audience with verses by Campoamor or scenes from 'Don Juan Tenorio' which he chose himself. It was a top-drawer cinema, and cost one peseta. It had the best class of audience, and the cinema was always full.

Perhaps with the passing of the years, my grandmother's memory embellished things, and I later learned that the most luxurious cinema was the Vedado. At first it was only open on Saturdays and Sundays then slowly increased the number of nights it showed films. It had boxes down both sides, but there was considerable chaos since the audience moved around as it pleased and could even use folding chairs in the stalls. Families took out season tickets to their favourite box; she and Evaristo had No. 9.

It was in the Vedado cinema that I saw the first full-length feature films. They were French, and were called The Black Pearl, A Trip to the Moon, *and* Goat's Foot. *My memory is confused: it mixes mediaeval castles, long-haired pages, girls sitting on golden stars against a dark blue background. They were in colour; if I'm not mistaken they coloured them in. Max Linder, and later Camilo del Pozo, performed all kinds of stunts, running in and out of the same door more often than a greyhound. Respectable men laughed their heads off and people hit each other in the face with imitation cream cakes, or Apaches wiped everybody out. I used to bite my nails, hold my hands to my mouth, and cry buckets, but I loved it and hated missing Saturday nights and Sunday matinées.*

Chapter Thirty-Two

DOLORES WAS GOING TOO FAR. That she put his marriage at risk, he could still handle; that on Sunday afternoons she went to the Malecón with musicians, poets and vulgar Galicians was not very convenient but one day he might benefit from that rabble's votes; but what he could not tolerate were meetings under his own roof with leaders of the rebellion, friends of Monguita. What an unexpected strategy on the part of the movement! Who would expect those dogs to hatch their plots in the house of the tiger? If the police found out, it would be his downfall, with prison included. He would wriggle out of it somehow, but she would face the firing squad.

For purely family reasons, insisted Don Mario, without going into the political consequences, she must go back to Spain to give birth and stay until the child was grown.

'Go for a couple of years. The climate is much better for a baby, and when you come back I'll be able to find you some fulfilling occupation.'

I SAID NOTHING. I just listened. Initially I understood nothing of plantations, surplus value and revolution, which came up so often in Evaristo's conversations with Monguita. I pretended I knew, remembering Miragaya's advice: 'Still waters run deep'. Then I would go and look up the words in the library's encyclopaedia.

On one of their outings, Evaristo took her to visit a shack in La Víbora, a poor neighbourhood of La Habana. The negroes used to practise religious rites and rituals centred around the spirituality of the natural world, in which these descendents of Africans still believe. The ancestral divinities still live in Africa, spirits that the negroes fear and venerate as they did in the days of the slave trade, and on whose hostility or benevolence all their successes and failures depend.

Women had to content themselves with being spectators at *ñáñigo* feasts. They were held, only for the initiated, in the woods or on waste ground after the ritual ceremonies. Lola was allowed to attend a funeral courtesy of a venerable *abasí*, dressed in palm fibre trousers tied at the waist. The last rites were performed for the deceased on the site where years ago a *ceiba* tree had stood. A dead cock on a roof tile, with something human and sad about it, represented the departed *abakuá*.

'We negroes are not like you, who spend your life praying and meditating. For us prayers are musical. Through song and dance, we conjure up the rain, we give thanks for the end of an epidemic, we flee malignant spirits and we ask the souls of the departed for a good harvest.'

The Begetter of life received us.

'We are children of the forest, because that's where life began. Our saints and our religion were also born in the forest.'

Then Sandoval, the medicine man, an elderly descendent of Egwedós, stressed:

'Everything comes from the forest; we must beg the forest for everything, for it gives us everything.'

From this explanation and other similar ones, I deduced that Forest means Earth, Universal Mother.

'In the forest live the *Orishas*: Elegguá, Oggún, Ochosi, Oko, Ayé, Changó, Allagguna,' added the medicine man. 'And Eggún, Eleko, Ikus, Ibbayes. It is full of the departed.'

The rainmaker puts water and healing roots in a gourd. He stirs them with a stick that he turns as if he wants it to catch fire. He froths up the liquid like a fluffy cloud and sprinkles it in every direction, like a bishop from Mondoñedo, swab at the ready. Then he burns other herbs which give off black vapours, puts them in the aforementioned water, and the cinders give off more and more steam. The clouds grow darker as the rainmaker keeps stirring with his magic stick; whirlpool turns to whirlwind that turns to rain clouds.

THE DANCERS SETTLE THEMSELVES on the ground; there is no leader, nor set dance. Unconnected notes emerge and are transformed into melody. The other musicians set the tempo and the tone. The dancers stand where they wish, make rhythmic movements, shaking their heads in time to the music. Gradually they seem to be intoxicated by the cadence, which gets faster and faster, accelerating at regular intervals, becoming more and more demonic, moving in a trance until they reach a real frenzy.

The uniform tempo at which they jumped, twirled and twisted was astonishing. The rhythms followed on seamlessly, one after another, increasingly fast and noisy, until the final apotheosis. Dancers and spectators both were left gasping. Then suddenly the music and dancing stopped; the dancers rigid in their last positions. For a few seconds, absolute silence reigned.

Nothing, no noise, no breathing. Then the drums start again, double in number and intensity. As eyes grow accustomed to the dark, a woman appears, in a skirt of palm leaves, nude from the waist up. She stands stock still in the centre of the circle, on her head a crown of zebra mane, two strips of skin across her breasts and arms. A fringe of cloth covers the front of her thighs, and hangs down to her ankles at the back.

She came and stood beside me, her whole face illuminated in the darkness by the two glowing coals of her eyes, like those of a tiger that gleam in the night and, it is said, lead the way to death and destruction.

'No doubt you lost your way tonight and accidentally stumbled upon this place, from whence leaving intact is the best of the mercies you can expect. Because you are in open country here, we have only to utter a single cry and four thousand spirits will come and carry you away. But that is not the fate awaiting you.'

The dancer began to move her hips by shaking her belly, and by so doing, slowly, edged towards me. She led me into the circle, and I, overwhelmed by a feeling of infinite tension and greatness, could no longer think, or know how to act. She took off my light bodice and clutched me against her, skin to skin. I noticed she was smeared with a paste-like substance which held us together, and we began to dance in unison. The drums and guttural cries of the musicians intensified. Joined to the dancer, I followed the tempo of her feet, her shuddering and convulsions. We calmed down slowly like Siamese twins, but to the same throbbing beat of the drums, and detached ourselves, our skin sticking painfully, as if we were leaving half of each other's bodies behind. Old women embalmed us with plant extracts and we lay exhausted for I don't know how long, until the timpani faded away.

'Tell me the oath you wish me to make for you. The one you think commits and binds you most, and I will not come to you until you feel the need, and tell me, "Go, let us start fighting." Swear to me, by He who put souls in bodies and created the laws of the Universe, that you will not use this power except for good, and in cases of extreme need.'

By all the saints! No priest, not even the Pope of the Catholics, made me swear an oath, or impose one of such gravity on me.

Nonetheless, she gives the dancer the oath she asks for and follows her indications as to how to swear it, then sinks into the sea of reflections.

'In truth, your request is something I have never granted anyone, and your destiny has willed it. But I would ask you one favour.'

'What is it?'

'Stay with me like this for fifteen minutes, breath to breath, pulses and heartbeats in unison. I will help the other Lola you carry within you to emerge, and both of you, like all beings that are chosen, will set out to walk parallel paths.'

I read something unimaginable in the dancer's face. I felt too weak to walk. And to discover what I felt that night I would have to read, who knows, all the stories in the world for a thousand and one nights.

SHE WALKED FOR A COUPLE OF HOURS, step after automatic step, till she reached her door. She found it locked and lay down in the doorway, so discouraged she did not know what was happening around her. Soon Monguita came out, and taking her in her arms, she carried her to bed.

She took care of me until I recovered. Then I threw myself in her arms and told her all about the dancer, from beginning to end, the way she had held me tightly to her body, and I had done nothing to extricate myself.

'Cheer up, my girl, leave your troubled mind behind. Go home for a year, or two, or three, until your breast fills with joy and your spirits rise. Mother Yemanyá willed that you live and see your homeland again. The sailors are busying themselves preparing the voyage and the boat will leave here in three days for one of the ports in Galicia. From there, in three days on foot, you can reach your village of Lanzós, where your mother is waiting to see you before she dies.'

'Not before time, Monguita. Since the day I left my country, I've had tears in my eyes and a heavy heart. I have not known if I would get the chance to see the land of my birth again and die beside my mother, and, if the truth be known, I'm tired of all that I have lived in this vale of tears. And also, Monguita, the dancer told me something I must cherish.'

'When Changó appears to you, control bids you farewell. You have the gift of ubiquity, a unique and terrible gift at the same time. It is a power you cannot pass on; it lies dormant within you and you don't know when it will come out. You will have to defy the gods!'

Chapter Thirty-Three

DON MARIO ARRANGED EVERYTHING with geometric meticulousness. We are in our sixth month and it is becoming a scandal. The Alfonso XII *is sailing for Vigo in three days. The ticket had to be bought at least twenty-four hours before; in second class, my son will not be travelling in the 'Court of Miracles' with the Galician riffraff. We said goodbye, pregnancy to boot, while his trusting wife was having her siesta.*

PRESIDENT JOSÉ MIGUEL GÓMEZ was a Liberal party politician, and had been a general in the Independence War. When he became President, the situation for workers and peasants did not change much, despite the fact the economic conditions had improved and the price of sugar was back to normal.

The Liberal and Conservative parties alternated in political power, just like the Spain of Cánovas and Sagasta. In both cases, the governing tribes of Generals and Doctors had not the slightest social conscience. For these patricians, the problems of workers and peasants were as far removed from them as Siberia. They considered the anarchists, destroyers of the apparatus of the state, their mortal enemies. When the Liberal Party was in opposition, however, its most progressive elements tried to attract the anarchists with small favours, like legal defences or deferential articles in their press, more in order to manipulate them than out of real sympathy. For their part, the Conservatives devoted themselves to hunting them down and in less than ten months managed to deport about two hundred of them.

THEY WALK DOWN THE SILENT and still-deserted street. The front gates of the mansions are closed and the blinds drawn in the basements where the servants live, as well as at the windows of the upper floors the masters inhabit. On the corner, the night watchman wrapped in his cloak with a lantern and ring of keys, waits patiently for the night to end.

They were all Galicians. I don't recall a single Cuban or Chinese policeman, night watchman, or lamplighter. The latter were agile and punctual, lighting the gas lamps with long poles, and I think I remember them carrying a little ladder over their shoulders. But I never saw them put out a lamp. I suppose they put them out in the morning, because I don't think the lamps put themselves out.

WHEN WE REACH THE MALECÓN, little sparks of sun begin to break up the grey of the waters. In the bay, ships of the Spanish Royal Navy lie at anchor. The morning awakes and stirs, the port springs to life. Tousled heads throw buckets of water into the sea. Free negroes who work on the docks, arrive in gangs of coloured stripes. A group of peninsula Spaniards, now rich, are returning home.

Monguita did not want me to go back to Galicia. She said I would be very useful to them in the coming crisis. Evaristo thought so too. When we reached the port and saw the name of the boat, we looked at each other and hesitated: it symbolised the massacres of the mambís *fifteen years earlier. Suddenly, as if a tombstone had dropped from the sky, all three of us thought of the climate of obscurantism awaiting me in Galicia and in which my son would have to be educated. And who knew if I would ever come back to Cuba? The ticket Don Mario had bought me was one-way. Surely a ruse to be rid of me, said Monguita to enlighten me:*

'You're being forced to return to your land. Hens don't vote in a fox's courtroom. Go now. But remember this, a bird that deserts a country, leaves part of itself behind.'

SECOND-CLASS PASSENGERS travelled with fleas, bedbugs and a cabin for two people of the same sex but who did not know each other. Dolores's companion was a soprano from an opera company who had just performed for two nights in Cuba. They lunched at a cloth-covered table, ate with a fork, and killed time with card games like *brisca, tute* and even baccarat, if anyone was inclined to gamble.

La Habana was an obligatory stopover for opera or theatre companies en route for New York. They stopped on the way there to give some show or other which served as a dress rehearsal. They stopped on the way back to help cover the costs of such an expensive journey from Europe.

In those days the *Nacional* theatre put on the most brilliant seasons one could wish to see, with singers like Titta Ruffo, Hipólito Lázaro, Enrico Caruso or María Barrientos. And because of the rate of exchange with the dollar, they were contracted for sums that were risible in the US but exorbitant in Europe.

However, the singers did not know what they were getting into. The Nacional *had an entrance worthy of a regional music hall, not of a theatre of that importance. Beside it were two premises rolled into one: one to exhibit Spanish cultural wares; and another with a band playing typical* charanga *music. Caruso could be singing 'La donna è mobile' backed by the massed ranks of the orchestra, while the audience were actually hearing street sounds and the Cuban band because doors and windows were left open due to the heat. Also joining the chorus were six lions from a circus which spent their nights in the neighbouring cellar and did nothing but yawn and roar. To make the racket even worse, crowds came to see Cuba's first luminous advertisement nearby: a huge green frog blinking in front of a slogan saying: 'Water is for breeding frogs in, so drink La Campana gin.'*

Dolores had been with Chané to several operas under these conditions, and had admired tenors and divas like the one she now shared a cabin with.

THE OPERA COMPANY WAS RETURNING from making its debut in *La Fanciulla del West* at the New York Metropolitan Opera House directed by Toscanini, with Emmy Destinn and Enrico Caruso in the principal roles. Dolores's cabin companion was called Elvira. She was the wife of Giacomo Puccini. The singers in the chorus warned her to watch out for Elvira's paranoid obsession: that every single woman was in love with her husband and wanted to take him away from her. They told the story of a girl from the village of Torre del Lago where Puccini lived with his family. A seventeen-year-old called Doria Manfredi had entered their service. Elvira immediately became violently and then unhealthily jealous. After four years she managed to throw Doria out, but continued to accuse her of having relations with her husband. So much so, that the girl committed suicide that same year. The autopsy proved her virginity, her family sued Elvira, who nevertheless kept on and on, until Puccini barred her from the company. The singers recommended Dolores talk to her as little as possible; they would try and get her into the choir, after an audition with the maestro.

What a strange man, Puccini. His desire to stay young was pathetic. Apparently Doctor Voronov had injected him with monkey glands to restore his youthful appearance. He was fifty and was already tormented by impotence and death.

The company had agreed to give a performance of the opera *a cappella* to cover the cost of their tickets. Puccini was furious because the programme had the year of his birth written in it. Since one day it would have to include the year of his death, he wanted the programmes withdrawn so he would not have to think about it. Dolores saw him about ten times, between tests and rehearsals. Singing the *Fanciulla's* folkloric melodies, pentatonic scales and syncopated rhythms without having heard them before, was difficult for her. So Puccini paid her more attention than the others and provoked his wife's rage. She insisted they change her cabin and throw her out of the chorus. The choir sided with the Galician girl and the passengers were left without their performance.

Chapter Thirty-Four

CUBA LOOKS LIKE A PLOUGH, doesn't it? Like the ones we call Roman ploughs in Galicia? Well, Cienfuegos is at about four hundred kilometres from La Habana on the south coast, between the point and the handle. Evaristo decided we would all make the journey there, but in separate groups. Black woman with white woman, Monguita with me, because something might happen to me on my own. And Evaristo with two other negroes nearby to protect us, just in case. However, because it would be ridiculous and suspicious for us not to speak for three days, he suggested we pretended to flirt. He was an expert at pretence because of living clandestinely. This helped us get to know each other better and the long journey was as delightful as the sea.

SHE HAD NEVER BEEN IN VIGO BEFORE. No one was expecting her. She went to the Hostal Berbés and calculated from memory how long the money Don Mario had given her would last: the mail-coach from Vigo to Compostela, five pesetas; the night in Compostela, two; another five from Compostela to Lugo; two *reales* from Lugo to Irimia, from there to Lanzós seven kilometres on foot, free as usual. She had five *reales* left for breakfast, lunch and dinner. If she did not fritter it, she could even buy a little present for her family.

EVERYTHING WAS THE SAME SHAMBLES in the Galicia I had left fifteen years ago; except in Lanzós. There, were the same shades of green, the same muddy pathways, and the identical disastrous grocer's shop. What made me most emotional was the song of the carts. The monody of two pieces of wood rubbing, the voice of the landscape itself; the lullaby of the tree, that dies with the day; the tapping of the stone breakers in their daily, slow, monotonous work, keeping time with a serene and infinite cadence. And above all, the smell of manure which in Cuba I missed so much.

For the rest, in so few years, *muñeira* music had disappeared; youths took advantage of new music to grope by; the bagpipes were replaced by a band with a vocalist; some bagpipe players wore regional costumes better suited for *churro* sellers; youngsters deserted the dusty atriums of the churches to go dancing on varnished dance floors.

Before I fled to Cuba, we would walk for hours and hours to run the smallest errand. By the time I came back, we had bicycles and some even had large cars which limped along the roads. The legions of beggars were less numerous. To reach the church before you had to pass through two lines of supplicants, more plaintive for their appearance than for their laments. It was probably pure disguise and make-up for the main part, although that did not make it any less unpleasant.

THE FIRST PERSON *I bumped into in Lanzós was Miragaya, greying but as phlegmatic and ironic as ever. It was as if I had kissed him the day before.*

'How are you, girlie? And how is Graciano?'

I hoped to find him here: it would have been so important to give my son a grandfather!

'That's bad luck! Didn't you see him in La Habana? Well, he went there. Years ago he sent me a letter with news of his landing in Cuba.'

> 'My dear Miragaya,
>
> I suppose you realised I would finally come back to La Habana, where most of my friends are and where I imagined I'd find Loliña. But you'll never believe what trials and tribulations I met before I reached the capital. To cut a long story short, when I arrived they put me in an internment camp, in a cell with a Chinaman, who

was actually a very nice person and helped me bear my imprisonment. I was taken out of there by the Galician Centre, thanks to Chané and Pondal, whose names I gave the camp guards.

When I came out, I learned that Independence and US intervention had rendered my property worthless. To survive I had to work hard in stalls and stores, and was even a foreman in sugar mills like my own! Finally, again with Pondal's help, I became a salesman peddling cloth door to door, toiling under a sun which made me sweat worse than a negro.

But I welcomed all these mortifications, because I finally bumped into Loliña in the street as she was coming out of the Galician Centre after choir rehearsal. Imagine my emotion. My whole body trembled, I could not say her name, nor did I dare address a word to her, with the way I looked and she so distinguished. We looked at each other and she said nothing, as if she did not know me. I found this normal, because of what I told you about my appearance, I looked like a criminal, a tramp, but I didn't have the means to dress better. I followed her from afar but she did not turn her head to look at me. She went into an aristocratic mansion from whence wafted a beautiful melody, played on a piano. I stayed there, waiting, listening to a habanera and seeing her move from one part of the house to another, very much at home. I realised I could not offer her such luxury and I accepted my lot. I felt happy to have known her and that in my old age she gave me illusions and hopes I had never imagined. What luck I did not listen to the advice you gave me. My life could end there. I could never reach a higher degree of contentment. And for now, the only compensation will be to go and listen to the ballad every day and see her. So, my dear Miragaya, I will not be coming back while I can work and be near Loliña.

Pray look after the little I left in Lanzós and protect my few belongings. To the contrary, I'll have to put everything in the hands of the mayor and his henchmen, and I would not like that at all.

A warm embrace from your friend,

Graciano

'Before he left, he deposited a will at the law court in Irimia. Go and ask to see it,' said Miragaya.

For Manuela, it was an unpleasant surprise. She imagined her daughter was well established but here she is back again, and in her belly a grandson, whose provenance she does not know, and whom she would probably have to look after.

'Don't worry, mother. What's important now is to see what we do with Graciano's inheritance.'

'He left you something?'

'Yes. I don't know how much. A few thousand.'

THERE WAS A LOT OF DISSATISFACTION among the negro population. The Independent Party of Colour tried to harvest fruit commensurate with its participation in the struggle for Independence, and complained that the traditional parties did not show solidarity with them. Nevertheless, Evaristo had determined followers among the construction workers and newspaper sellers in La Habana.

Nothing is more difficult than concealing love. Small gestures, tone of voice, furtive glances, betray more that futile displays of affection. Arm in arm with Monguita, I began to attend the rebels' meetings, and soon understood what one of our poets said, that everything is in the eye of the beholder. From the negroes' point of view, their life was not as transparent as we maintained. Their masters had co-opted the rule of law and they, who had won the war, had come second in everything: work, education, and health. Their children were dying of hunger yet they no longer even hung their hopes on old-style paternalism; the State managed to block all ways out of their predicament.

They were at an event in Camagüey. To warm up the audience, before giving his speech, Estenoz told the story of the wife of Chief Guamá. A prisoner of the Spanish, and about to be executed, Casiguaya – that was her name – roused the other prisoners with the cry '*Manicato!*' which in her tongue meant courage, bravery. When it was her turn to die, however, she said she was prepared to renege, denounce, and betray her own people, if they would allow her to embrace her four-year-old daughter. After this favour was conceded, she pretended to caress the child and strangled her as she cried '*Manicato!*' She then jumped into the noose to hang herself. With her last breath, Casiguaya gave her executioners one final warning: 'Neither wife nor daughter of Guamá will be slaves!'

'This anecdote goes to show that the fighting spirit of Cuban women comes from way back into our history,' concluded Estenoz.

I thought it an act of savagery to kill her daughter for so little, and no matter how revolutionary I was I would never do it. My thoughts were interrupted because my man continued:

'What the hell did they imagine, that we would surrender like tame sheep, that we would hand over our weapons and give up? Absolutely not. And we showed them. They called us savages, patent-leather blacks and a thousand more insults. But when has anyone ever had a more democratic programme than that of the Independents of Colour? When has anyone ever fought tooth and nail to obtain benefits for negroes, who fought in the war, barefoot, in rags, and hungry, like Quintín Banderas himself, who they then killed as he was drawing water from his well? Don't let them come to us with idle talk. Now is the time for justice. And none of us who risked our skins in that war are going to keep our mouths shut. At least, anyone who comes to where I'm standing and talks about racism, about blacks being bloodthirsty, I'll give him such a bloody nose he'll know who Esteban Montejo is.'

At the end of the meeting the crowd dedicated a ditty to Evaristo. I remember it because I sang it a lot afterwards to make fun of him:

This brave general
of colour independent
Is our tropical emperor
and our next president.
To see him like this,
his uniform so brilliant,
We have to say
we're with you, commandante.

I listened and digested it all, in open-mouthed admiration for such a fiery speech, and that's how Monguita and the others realised the intensity of our relationship. They noticed it in our behaviour. Monguita was more affectionate than ever and the party members more deferential.

Then Ivonet took the stage:

'Black woman may beget black, white woman may beget white, but they are both mothers, so says our wise refrain. We are all equal. Nonetheless, we negroes occupy a very distinguished place in the struggle for independence. Céspedes, who represented the interests of the *Criollo* landowners, freed his own slaves and incorporated them into the ranks of the revolutionary army. It was not long before other masters freed theirs too. All were negroes. The triumph of the Revolution depended on the speed with which they could recruit the greatest possible numbers throughout the island and organise an army. For instance, Antonio Maceo, the people's idol during the Revolution, was a negro. He rose from being a simple soldier to Lieutenant General and second in command of the Liberation Army before his death in combat. His father and nine brothers were also killed, or wounded. I'll also mention Generals Quintín Banderas, Flor Crombet, Guillermo Moncada and Agustín Cebreco, all great negro leaders. Then there were no white Cubans and black Cubans, nor regiments for whites only, we were all Cubans. The backbone of the Liberation Army was negroes. We represented seventy per cent of the army, although we were only a third of the population.'

When the meeting ended, the audience sang another couplet for Ivonet:

Here stands Ivonet
fair-haired Cubo-Frenchman,
And rebel leader that he is
he puts Spaniards in a jam.
He wears a Haitian uniform
of his rank and position
And thinks one day he'll be
a field marshal Afro-Cuban.

Chapter Thirty-Five

THE THOUSANDS INHERITED FROM GRACIANO turned out to be a few miserable sovereigns, not enough for Dolores to move to the capital, but enough to restore the grocer's shop, along the lines of her mother's strange notions. Manuela's supreme art, intact at her sixty-odd years, was making a silk purse out of a sow's ear. After much deliberation, she convinced herself that fate had willed that her daughter return to her, now the time was nigh for her to fulfil her mission. Dolores accepted her destiny, sensing she had lost none of her knowledge of witchcraft. On the contrary, Cuba had heightened her contact with the Anointed. Mother and daughter decided to establish a consultancy of esotericism in what was formerly the grocer's. It took a couple of months to clear the undergrowth, refurbish the shop's interior and whitewash the facade. And to avoid suspicion and keep in with the Church, they created an enigmatic and ambiguous sign:

SANTA EIRÍA
Miraculous Cures

Culitrenzado had sighed his last sigh. After Graciano's departure, the ass had been left without an owner. The parish priest in his mercy fitted out a corner of the sacristy for him. But that was all he did for him, he spent not a penny more. For days and days he pulled the cart, without a bite to eat, until he died a natural death. 'What bad luck,' sighed Don Gabriel. 'He died on me just as he had got used to fasting.'

The choirboys sang couplets alluding to the priest's miserliness:

The priest has lost the beast
Because he did not feed him barley.
Now he goes to a funeral feast
On his housekeeper's pony.

It is time to recognise the virtues of that unique and patient animal that lived through hungry times in Lanzós without ever complaining, kicking or braying. Nor did he tell anybody the secret poem of his dreams, in which the memory of his species relived the nuzzling, jumping, and endless pathways where ancestral asses frisked and frolicked, because he had never known chemically modified fodder, nor luxury stables, nor had he read the treatise of Professor of Agriculture Horacio Nobet, which was to become the Zootechnia Bible.

So, Dolores set off again on the rounds of the country fairs in the same carriage, more ramshackle yet with more charm. The same old blind man, guided by the same little girl (twenty years on), sang the same ballads written on the same various coloured sheets, in a voice like a goat.

They robbed her of two reales
That she had kept hidden.
And not content with this
That dreadful scoundrel
Took her to the balcony,
Threw her from the window
Where she fell on her face
Into the heap of manure.
When she sees she is dead,
She turns over on her back
And they fill her mouth
With manure from the stable.

THE FRATRICIDAL STRUGGLE intensified. The Independent Party of Colour's most implacable opponents – various negro leaders well established in the Liberal Party – spread the rumour that Estenoz was receiving money from the Conservatives to prevent them getting votes. He denied it, saying his party took votes from Liberals and Conservatives alike. 'White people in general are enemies of the negroes, who until now had no one looking out for their interests. The Republic should belong to everybody.'

It was also said that Evaristo's party was trying to get the Americans to intervene. In fact Yankee warships had arrived in Cuba in those very days. They were the results of the contacts Evaristo and I had made in the US!

DOLORES'S TALK OF THOUSANDS had been absentminded; she had been away from Spain so long that she confused pesos, pesetas, dollars and sovereigns. All the same, her mother's attitude to her changed. The task of tending the cows now passed exclusively to her sister, although Dolores would have found it fairer to take turns. But her mother wanted her to attend sorcery sessions more often. In exchange for notions of *Santería*, she received secrets of popular Galician folklore, with which she created a syncretism of her own, all the more acceptable in Galicia where a large number of *indianos* espoused *Ñáñigism*, African pagan rituals.

She accompanied her mother on visits to cripples and was beside her in witchcraft consultations. To children who had the evil eye on them she prescribed cures from her own esoteric beliefs.

If you look at children while they are sleeping, they wake up cross-eyed; worse still, if someone with the evil eye watches them, it could turn them blind. To immunise them against the evil eye – since children are more vulnerable than animals – give them a piece of coral when they are born. For adults, I recommend a ring with a cat's-eye gem.

Dolores made friends with the girl who guided that same judge whom Graciano had blinded, accompanying him from fair to fair, and assisting him by pointing to a board showing the images her master sang about in his ballads.

I told her how I had fled Galicia, what I had experienced and learned so far from home, and it moved her greatly. She brought me newspaper cuttings about crimes and scandals so we could make up verses for her master to sing. One of my songs, the first to be published in pamphlet form, although I wrote many in my lifetime, began like this:

Among your fields and flowers
Under a boundless sky
I enjoyed the warbling
Of your song birds
And your river of crystal

At sunset I would pass the places where blind people stood, and could not help stopping to listen to my own tales, which on their lips sounded all the more moving. Such was the effect the songs had on people that I ended up crying like everybody else. And I discussed the sorrowful tales with the audience, without them knowing I wrote them. But let it be clear, I am no writer, or rather, I wasn't then. I wrote those poems without ever having read one. I always hoped to recover the luxury edition of poetry that Curros Enríquez gave me a few days after we first met. I lost it in one of those Santería rituals, among all that shaking that went on.

Chapter Thirty-Six

DURING THE DAY I HAD TALKED to Monguita a lot about the attacks committed by certain groups of Independents infiltrated by the Yankees. Afterwards, when Evaristo and I went home, we discussed the validity of these actions, and whether any of our followers would be involved. Evaristo said no, but I was not so sure. At night I was assailed by two dreams, separate but linked by a sound. I had been to look for Mama at the fair in Montforte but could not find her. I was coming home when she pulled my sleeve and said, 'I'm here, Dolores.' Immediately afterwards I heard bells toll; softly at first, then more and more loudly; black iron bells, nearby in the night, until they all merged in a noise that culminated in a huge clap of thunder. I woke up with a start. Evaristo made me one of his potions to calm me, but I could not get back to sleep.

HER MOTHER WAS GETTING OLD, fading like the light of a candle. Since no doctor or priests helped witches to die, she was accompanied by Miragaya's sobbing and the resignation of her daughter, who grieved as she listened to her last words.

'Know, my child, that my life is drawing to an end, and the moment is nigh for me to move to a more permanent home. I will depart this world leaving you with child; but I tell you now that you will give birth to a son and you will call him Xosé, for me. And you will give him a good upbringing, so that when he is grown and asks you, "What did my father leave me," you can answer, "goodness and knowledge".'

Soon afterwards, the church bells began to toll for her.

Church bells in Galicia have numerous inflections and ringing patterns: common death knolls; clapper rolls for poor parish priests; and multiple rounds for important clerics (canons or bishops). Peals of bells invite to weddings or announce births, one chime for boys, another for girls. For babies, the rhythm changes as the birth approaches, from the initial proclamation bell until the joyous peal if the outcome is happy or, to the contrary, a toll parodying the *dies irae* *that accompanies the little angel into limbo. For His Holiness I don't think there was a partiture, since Popes die once in a blue moon and it takes months for news from Rome to arrive in Lanzós.*

THANKS TO THE *INDIANOS*, who went to and from Cuba, the two parts of Dolores exchanged grief and joy, so that their heart mourned their reciprocal absences. One of the travellers brought Dolores in Galicia a little packet from Dolores in La Habana, with amulets and such a beautifully written letter that Dolores thought it was Evaristo's hand, not noticing that Dolores now wrote very well. She now understood the enigmatic words of the Yoruba dancer and that she now had that gift of ubiquity granted to her, which she had forgotten, and how terrible it would be to bear. Dolores recounted her latest adventures on the island:

> How sad, Dolores, these noon times without you! Cockroach coloured sky, yellow rain, birds that flit between the bell ropes and swoop squawking from the bell towers. Both Evaristo and I feel your absence and miss you sadly. The Movement continues and has had pleasing successes. The negroes are increasingly angered by the contempt in which they are held by the Liberals, who they helped so much and in whom they had such high hopes. But you see, if you don't suck you don't feed, so pray to God and wield a machete. A young Dominican girl of barely twenty called Camila Salomé Henrique has joined our group and never leaves our side. Just imagine, she and I are studying French. I already understand many of those strange disconcerting words: chapeau, déjeuner, and fromage mean hat, lunch and cheese. We never stop learning. Very tall, upright, and with nobility and great personal

charm, Camila makes the others follow paths that she herself charts; she knows how to reach them and transmit the justice of the cause. I find her comparisons very amusing. According to her, we women are either old maids, prostitutes, married or widowed. That is, for centuries, with the complicity of our laws and traditions, more than half the inhabitants of the world have been prevented from leading a life that is useful to humanity and to themselves. It gives me much food for thought. The first battle we must win is to liberate ourselves. Yankees, racism and everything else would disappear from our world. I don't know if I'm explaining it properly. With this ñáñigo, I'm sending you some magazines in which Salomé talks about it. You are as learned as I, so you will understand it. Keep in good health and know that we wait for you always.

A warm embrace, DOLORES

Chapter Thirty-Seven

THE MOVEMENT OF COLOUR was making strides, it is true, but Evaristo Estenoz and Pedro Ivonet had problems: no one knew who was backing the insurrection. The most widespread opinion was that it had been financed by large companies in order to get the Yankees to intervene and protect their own interests. The trips Estenoz made to the US came to light and the public thought the excessive benevolence with which the justice system had treated him was unacceptable. He was sentenced to a hundred and twenty days in prison for his articles in the newspaper *Previsión*. The conservative lawyer Freyre de Andrade defended him, and he and other leaders of his party were acquitted shortly afterwards. So, he was able to walk freely about La Habana, although he was advised to keep his eyes peeled.

These rumours did not reach Evaristo because he did not step outside his circle of admirers. For him, it was more important that both he and Ivonet be acclaimed by large numbers of negroes in Santiago, and that thirty-two thousand signatures had been collected in support of the abolition of the Morúa Amendment, which prohibited parties based on race. But I heard what white people were saying in the street, and especially the anarchists, since I spent a lot of time with them and they were very critical of our movement. Evaristo listened to me as if he were listening to rain fall. He said the opposite was true. The more successful the insurrection, the more detractors it would have.

Each time US warships arrived in La Habana, Estenoz wrote to the US Secretary of State denouncing the outrages Generals Gómez and Monteagudo committed against the negroes.

He didn't tell me himself, as he feared my criticism. I read it in the newspapers and began to believe the Independents of Colour were trying to justify armed intervention by the US. To me it was inciting the US to enforce the Platt Amendment. And I told him so bluntly, to which he replied with vacuous words.

'It is impossible to reach any kind of agreement with a government that does not deserve our trust. They only divide opinion within the country, trying to convince the whites we hate them and that our demands merely pit negroes against whites, and you know better than anyone that what we seek is exactly the opposite.'

I dreaded the course this racial hatred was taking, exacerbated by the rumours of attacks on white women and the articles denouncing negroes that appeared in the press. They resulted in a tragic incident in Regla. A group of whites had attacked some negroes suspected of helping the rebels; they defended themselves with weapons and a shoot-out ensued. Later, another crowd of whites lynched a negro and beat others they found as they were marauding round the streets of the town.

Chapter Thirty-Eight

MY CONTRACTIONS STARTED *the previous afternoon, at five-minute intervals. I hadn't felt anything before that, and had almost forgotten I would be a mother one day. Even now I don't think I was very aware of the fact. After a few hours I sent for the midwife, because I was alone in the house. She came and went. She told me to call her when I was about to give birth. Poor me, if I had not given birth before, how would I know when I was about to? They say it is very painful but I wasn't suffering at all. I did, however, hear perfectly well the murmurings of my body, and knew each contraction was massaging the baby outwards. I felt each one rise from the beginning of time, but was this it, being about to give birth? No, perhaps not. I had no confidence in myself, but the contractions encouraged me, my body was ready, the baby was ready, should I help it come out? I refused to measure the sensations. Feeling them was enough. I hid the pendulum clock, hearing only the tick-tock. In this way, the contractions seemed more regular and effective.*

The midwife came back but I did not go out to greet her, I was so happy talking to the tiny little bud with my body and heart. Nonetheless, I was glad she came back, her presence calmed me, although at this moment I would've liked no one to be between us; only it and me. I felt uncomfortable lying on the bed and also noticed the baby preferred the vertical position. The midwife made me walk round the room; the dog followed us thoughtfully, as if asking me what I was doing up at this hour.

The midwife asked if she could listen to the baby's heart. Of course. Good, it was beating well. I knew it, I felt it. I thought of the animals I had seen giving birth: the mares lie down with the deepest of breaths, the cats miaow and show their claws; and now I was going to give birth, growling like thousands of cats, mares and cows; I was like them, they give birth without any help from vets or anyone. The baby arrived with the dawn. A boy. He cried a little and looked at me in surprise. He licked my breasts, sucked a finger. The midwife went, and left us alone in the half light.

Dolores had chosen a girl's name. But it was 19th March, so he would be called Xosé. Miragaya took care of his education and found a teacher to teach him to count, read and write. He learned everything without difficulty, completely naturally.

Chapter Thirty-Nine

THE INEVITABLE UPRISING OF the Independent Party of Colour took place, but was put down in twenty days by government forces, who gave no quarter. Over three thousand negroes and mestizos were killed, and twelve whites died. Battle was joined at Yeguada. A battalion of Independents of Colour attacked a barracks where Evaristo was being held after being sold down the river for a handful of coins by a certain Paranada.

Facing the negroes are two hundred riflemen, weapons at the ready. A crowd pursues and surrounds them; the sound of running feet is heard. Many negroes are smiling, as if they are going on a picnic; some carry shotguns, others machetes. They reach the prison where many of their comrades are being held. It is a small concrete barracks with balconies on the walls. They start pushing the doors with one accord, as if an order had been given. Amid jeers and whistles, the commander refuses to hand over the keys. They charge the doors with wooden beams, the slats splinter and a negro demolishes them with an axe. Fifty men break in. 'Here's the key to the padlocks,' shouts a rebel, and lets the others in.

So, fifty negroes attack. The soldiers present arms. Prisoners in an open cell stand trembling. Through the bars a dying face appears. 'These are not them,' the guards say, obsequiously, 'these are not them, they're upstairs, in the women's section, the other key is up there.' 'Slowly, gentlemen, slowly,' says the second-in-command. Who knows Estenoz? Only the negroes do! They run down the empty corridor. An African hand, scaly, ancient, blackish, points to the corner where the stairs are, where feet are flying. 'Hurrah, three hurrahs!' shouts one of the Independents. 'There he is.' Shots are heard. The soldiers advance upon the cells. They kill Bujalance on his knees, his forehead on the flagstones.

Bujalance's hat is torn to shreds, his frockcoat from the back in corduroy tatters. Another shot, the last from the fleeing soldiers, and a prisoner leaps into the air from a bullet in the brain. 'Long live Estenoz!' The other prisoners have no time to beg for mercy. 'On the ground!' Bienvenido and García lie riddled with bullets. Bullets fly. Estenoz, cornered, falls from a blow to the head. He dies there between the soldiers' feet, not a single shot, battered with rifle butts. Outside a terrible anger arises. 'Bring him out to us!' The square and the streets around are full. There are women and children. 'Bring him out! Out here!'

A platoon of soldiers appears dragging Paranada, the mad Judas. They drop him. Some hang the rope around his neck. Two of them wage a ferocious battle to decide which of them is to pull the noose tighter. Those nearby spit on him. Trickles of saliva run down his chest. Warm with death, the noose of the new rope is pulled. He is left hanging from the branch of a tree: the other branches are cut and women and children will wear the leaves in their hats, the men in their lapels, as a reminder of the treachery.

Chapter Forty

Dear Dolores,

How wise I was to undertake this long and arduous journey! And I congratulate myself for having extricated myself from the tight corner I was in. When I remember my troubles, my hair stands up on the back of my neck in fright. I thank the gods for having brought me back across the ocean, two thousand miles from you, to greet the land where we were born. I can't tell you how moved I felt to be back in the village where we took our first steps. Each object I see brings back memories of my childhood, and I am overwhelmed by some sense of mad and wild happiness that moves me to tears. I could kiss all the women, and the men. I like everything: the potatoes, the fruit, the birdsong. To these voluptuous memories are added the enchanting surprise I felt at seeing that mediaeval village, preserved intact in the modern age, and its unique customs we find both in Galicia and in the Americas: the funerals, the tales of apparitions, the relationship between life and death, those low houses with wooden balconies, windows with iron railings, all open in the summer, and the simple, clean rooms.

Xosé is growing up quite normally and I do everything I can to see he doesn't have the miserable life I had at his age. He is very bright at school, and as soon as he is eight I am sending him to the seminary in Mondoñedo, not to become a priest, don't worry, but he will have a pleasant time there and finish his high school studies. That's how poor people do things here, because there is no other way for them to get an education.

And now for some bad news. Mama died suddenly but without pain, and Angelita became a nun and entered the Adoratrices convent. Graciano has disappeared. They say he spent two years in jail, from whence he was released by the judge whom he blinded, and who now has a song in his heart as he performs his role of troubadour.

I will write soon, my dear. Miragaya has just come in. He sends his greetings. We are trying to sort things out, because here the situation is really complicated too. Soon I'll tell you of the exciting things awaiting us.

Chapter Forty-One

WHENEVER MY GRANDMOTHER talked to me about Cuba, the conversation always turned to Joaquín the Chinaman; cook, coachman and, if necessary, nursemaid. He was a very kind, sweet man, always ready to render a service. I imagined him exactly as she described him, with his green suit and long pigtail.

He had arrived in Cuba at the end of the nineteenth century, a little before I did, to work as a stretcher-bearer for Doctor Alvite. Children took to him straight away; he showed them infinite patience. He had a very personal idea of medicine, despite working in the house of a reputed doctor. I was ill one day and Joaquín was sent to the pharmacy to fetch something to calm an upset stomach, as they used to say before they knew about indigestion. He goes and says , 'Lola ill. Tumac sole. I go phalmasy, get balm lub on alse.'

The Chinese replaced the Spaniards, real Peninsular ones or Galicians, as they called us in those days. Chinese grocers carried up to six baskets, one on top of the other, on the two ends of a pole. They sat at the entrances to houses and, with the patience of Job, spread out their wares. They were very endearing, those small neat figures with their black shoes, and their baggy clothes from Canton.

I remember their round conical hats and the bows on their pigtails sticking out from underneath it. They were out and about in the early mornings, shuddering under their merchandise, walking quickly, almost jumping. They smiled a lot, and their baskets were stocked with everything you could possibly need. At the end of each sale, those who could write – not very many – noted down the quantities on bits of paper full of little drawings. When they were paid – not very much – they said thank you with deep but not servile bows. They got a reputation for probity, and were, apparently, excellent husbands and even better fathers.

A COUP D'ÉTAT BY PRIMO DE RIVERA ended the Roaring Twenties and installed his dictatorship.

At first we did not notice much difference. News of events in Catalonia would not reach Galicia until months later, so imagine what it would be like in Lanzós, where life carried inexorably on. From the Voz de Galicia, we learned that the dictator had a disproportionate admiration for Benito Mussolini, 'The apostle of the fight against anarchism'. But since there were no anarchists in our village, not that I knew of, I only feared for Durruti. From time to time we got news of his adventures in Argentina, where he was called a bandit.

Little by little the repression began to be felt. The number of censored newspaper articles increased, and those that were allowed only contained banalities. A national militia was formed, recruiting young men under thirty. Political parties were banned and mayors, previously elected by the people, were appointed by the government.

In Irimia, they designated José Fraga Bello, who after having been a farm hand in both Castile and Cuba, made the leap up to local chief of the CEDA, the Spanish Confederation of the Autonomous Right. Many rumours circulated about him, including the one that his son Manuel had prepared him to be mayor by teaching him to read and write. The truth is that in our area he began the period they called 'Regeneration'. He was very tall and upright, well dressed and stuffy. He inspired respect for his office and his bearing. It was said that he, together with the notary's secretary, and a certain Maceda, made decisions on anything to do with immigrants' inheritances.

THE FIRST YEARS AFTER MY RETURN, I devoted to Xosé's education. Miragaya had learned sums and rudiments of grammar as he was teaching his pupils. He passed it on to my son. With the help of Don Gabriel, warm and fun-loving as ever but with a good many extra years, we bought him a shabby cassock. He looked like a somewhat sinister altar boy, and seeing him like that made my flesh crawl. But I knew it was only for seven years, and he would come back bearing a school certificate. As for me, perhaps because of my orphan's complex, he revived the affection I felt for Graciano or the illusion of being close to the church, and by extension to Xosé. Whatever the reason, I resumed the clandestine relationship with the parish priest I told you of before. He was a different man from that brand new priest I had violated over fifteen years earlier.

On one of the many days he spent travelling from parish to parish to inspect the rectories, the Bishop of Mondoñedo, Monsignor Juan José Solís y Fernández, arrived in Lanzós. Don Gabriel's nervousness was touching. He was solicitous to a tee: Your Excellency here, Monsignor there, attentive to the prelate's every word or gesture, outdoing himself to satisfy his every need and showing him places that compromised him the least. But the inquisitive churchman kept asking questions.

'Do you live here alone, Don Gabriel?'

'No, not exactly…'

'And with whom do you live?'

'Well, my housekeeper is in the house as well. She makes my food, mends my clothes, does my washing and ironing…'

'And where the devil does she sleep, since I only see one bed?'

'We have to sleep together, Your Grace.'

'Together!'

'Yes, but we put a bolster between us…'

'A bolster! And what happens if you have a sinful urge?'

'Well, we take the bolster away.'

After further questioning, the investigating cleric discovered that I could sew and to protect the Church's honour, and hide the fact that Don Gabriel and I were living in sin, he arranged for me to make all the cassocks, birettas, surplices, and altar cloths for the liturgical ceremonies held in the bishopric. I was able to set up a sewing workshop in the Carmelite nunnery employing three cloistered nuns, who by giving me free access to their institution did not break the rules of their order; no nunnery could be more secluded than the one in Lanzós. This provided me with more than enough to rent a little house with two bedrooms, one for my son and one for me, with a back door so Don Gabriel could come whenever he wanted to confess his sins.

Chapter Forty-Two

THE TIME FOR REPARATION HAD COME, after a century of absolutism under the colonial yoke and fifteen years of an occupied Republic. Due to the trade conditions during the First World War, Cuba went through a period of seemingly endless well-being. Production increased: almost fifty new sugar mills began operating between 1913 and 1920. The provinces of Camagüey and Oriente developed intensively and fast. The price of sugar reached an all-time high, benefitting both landowners and farmers renting land, although the lot of farm labourers remained the same as in colonial times. The railways clocked up nine thousand kilometres of track, journeying through Cuba at thirty-five or forty kilometres an hour. It was an era known as the 'Dance of the Millions'.

Perplexed and confused, the Cubans were not prepared for excess or behaving like badly brought-up children. Money came into their purses and went out just as easily. Potentates appeared all over the island, so did populist strongmen and a myriad of nouveau riche landowners who did not know how to tie a tie, or phone their merrymaking cronies.

The plantation owners modernised their mills to increase their dividends and move to La Habana. Others, less ambitious, sold their lands and factories for unimaginable prices. The first thing they did with their money was buy a mansion of dubious taste in Vedado, and a car, even though they could not drive, since that is what negro chauffeurs in uniform were for. In this period of 'fat cows', the anarchists decided to remain neutral in the First World War, and hence were accused of being Germanophiles.

I spent a lot of time with anarchists ever since Evaristo had given me the job of liaising with them, but I was beginning to feel ill at ease, perhaps

because of their neutrality since I don't like doing things half-heartedly.
They established the Working Man's Club at No. 2 Egido Street in La
Habana, and it soon became the most popular left-wing meeting place.
For a whole decade, strikes, boycotts and country-wide activities were
organised from there. The general climate of upheaval had some tragic
consequences. Spanish and US economic interests, in cahoots with the
government, viewed any social protest or demonstration as a potential
outbreak of civil war. Enrico Caruso was charging ten thousand dollars
for each appearance, so one night a bomb exploded at the Opera House
during a performance of Aida. *Caruso fled in terror, followed by a group*
of anarchists. A policeman saw him and detained him for being on the
street in disguise outside Carnival time. 'Io non sono dizfrazato, sono
Enrico Caruso vestito de Radamés,' *he explained to the policeman in*
bastardised Spanish. 'With lipstick and rouge? Well, io sono Garibaldi
and I'm arresting you for being a queer.'

Chapter Forty-Three

WITH GRACIANO'S INHERITANCE, her savings from Cuba, and what she earned from her business in the nunnery, Dolores founded a cultural club where first the grocery store and then the Santa Eiría had been. She called it The Star, because of her sympathies with the Bolshevik Revolution. Miragaya was appointed caretaker, as was to be expected. Anyone could go in, talk, and rail against the dictatorship. They organised poetry readings, book exchanges and sporting events, in fact any activity opposed to the dictatorship. Sitting round a decrepit Philips radio, men and women alike tortured their eardrums trying to interpret the programmes, always favourable to the Fascists.

We weren't communists. There were only a hundred or so of those in the whole of Galicia. So I don't know how they heard about us, but a month after we opened, we received La Antorcha, *published by sympathisers of socialist ideas.*

This sympathy led to the formation of various nuclei of militant Galician nationalists, socialists, and anarchists, but it would be years before they were consolidated into any party or, indeed, had any structure.

It was very strange, because I think Vigo only received fifteen copies of La Antorcha, *Compostela seven and Ourense had only one subscriber. We were among the first promoters of communism, or rather socialism as a socio-political system, long before the party had been founded.*

Not long after The Star was inaugurated, a young man called Ángel Castiñeira turned up in Lanzós. Born in the village, he had gone to sea when he was a child, and had sailed between Buenos Aires and Montevideo for several years. Nobody remembered him. Slowly he let it be known that he had had contact with anarchist groups in the Americas, and by the time he arrived in Lanzós, was already part of the libertarian movement in Barcelona, and was in fact fleeing the police.

He came and went, arrived and disappeared, his life was very mysterious, but when Ángel began to trust us, he would tell us where he had been, what he was involved in, and through him we gradually learned what was going on in the rest of Spain.

He told us of the many protests and demonstrations being held in Barcelona because of the growing number of reservists called up to fight in the war in Morocco. He had taken part in the popular uprising of the 1909 Semana Trágica *with its strikes, bomb attacks, fires, which culminated in a gigantic anticlerical riot. The crowd has gone out into the streets spontaneously, without ideology or leadership, to express its hardships and dissatisfaction. Here in Lanzós, we tried to organise rebellious acts and obstructed the trains transporting young Galicians to Morocco. About thirty of us went twice to Baamonde and managed to stop the convoys, but the station master immediately sent to Lugo for reinforcements and a couple of hours later two lorries full of soldiers arrived to disperse us.*

Clean-shaven and with a priestly air, Ángel was always ready to give his neighbours a helping hand in the fields, and gained the sympathy of all and sundry, good people and bad. When elections for a new mayor came round, we proposed Miragaya, but the reactionaries in Irimia preferred Castiñeira, so without them even realising it, the best man won.

XOSÉ DID NOT TURN OUT to be very studious, although he did pass his exams thanks to some ecclesiastical boxing of ears. But he was bright enough at eighteen to notice the country was being peppered with old jalopies needing fuel, and got his mother to finance a petrol station on the crossroads to Lugo and Ferrol, where the stage coaches stopped occasionally. In his spare time, he took to frequenting his neighbours' wives, gave Dolores a grandson with the wife of a civil guard, and built a hotel on the main road.

Don't put it like that, it isn't true. My Xosé is very intelligent, but he inherited from us the irreligious gene, and that's why he was thrown

*out of the seminary; his certificate in hand, all the same. He didn't go
on to university for financial reasons; the nuns didn't stretch that far. The
hotel was my idea, because I was wondering how to expand the space for
political meetings and conceal them by getting the nuns to work as maids
and cooks, and so they didn't get bored in the convent.*

Her son struggled to build the hotel; it never became a real
hotel, just stayed a hostel. After Dolores and Don Gabriel lent him
the minimum, he went to the town's usurers and began building.
At the end of each month he had to hide so as not to pay his
workmen's wages. He ended up owing them so much that they
kept working for free in the hope that one day they would be
paid. It was either that or nothing.

Chapter Forty-Four

MANY YEARS PASSED, things changed so much… but the images from that very important period of my life are engraved in my memory: the salons, the parties, waltzes and habaneras were replaced by the fox-trot introduced from the North. The musical revolution went hand in hand with that of automobiles, because when the war prevented European cars from being imported, Cubans favoured the American models. Already victorious in the private car market, they dared penetrate the leasing market with the Ford, a good cheap car, albeit ungainly. In the streets, mule-driven carts waged a losing battle against cars. Although on Sunday afternoons along the Prado, the famous Malanguita calmly carried on driving her coach, pulled by a nag that had little to envy Culitrenzado.

To echo the European conflict, the coachmen called themselves 'Allies' and the chauffeurs 'Germans'. To compete with the wheels of progress, the former lowered their tariff to ten cents, and the latter kept theirs at eight.

But the prosperity vanished without warning and the dance ended. The North Americans were said to have refused to buy the sugar harvest in revenge for the previous exorbitant prices, which meant disaster for the Kingdom of Plenty.

Constitutional guarantees were suspended in an attempt to create a climate of terror in public opinion. About eighty workers, dubbed the 'anarcho-syndicalist horde', were deported. Anarchist publications were proscribed and the Working Man's Centre was closed.

I was always astonished by the Cuban character: extraordinary, delicious, attractive beings, with the virtue of staying happy even in the midst of pain and suffering. Their playful side came to the fore in adversity. For example, The Electric Railway Company ran the first

trams in Camagüey, Santiago and La Habana. The Cubans made up
this ditty about it:

If you want to see my parlour
Come and visit me one day.
Just get on and ride the tram
You'll be joyful all the way.

Oh, how wonderful, how great
To shake and wiggle on the way.
With Pepe or with Antoñico
I'm happy to travel all the day.

Despite their trials and tribulations, so many funny things happened
on the trams; if you saw them you'd want to die laughing. Most Cubans
preferred to put a good face on a bad situation and in the streets they
would sing 'The Peanut Vendor', the popular rumba by Moisés Simons.
At the same time, the political in-fighting carried on apace. The Liberal José
Miguel Gómez led the popular masses while the Conservative Menocal,
on seeing his prestige decline, made an alliance with Alfredo de Zayas and
his handful of supporters.

The role played by the neighbours from the north exacerbated
the situation. Washington resorted to a policy of 'preventative
intervention' and appointed Enoch Crowder as special pro-consul
in Cuba. He arrived in La Habana Bay on board the gunboat
Minnesota. The boat returned to the US but Crowder installed
himself in the Hotel Sevilla to govern the country. Since he
had offered a loan of fifty million dollars, he reserved the right
to meddle in Cuban affairs, interfering in budget spending,
constitutional reform, the reserve bank, sales taxes, reforming the
national lottery and public works contracts – all under threat of
military intervention.

A cartoon in the weekly La Politica Cómica *showed Zayas sitting*
in front of his desk. Behind him, Crowder is guiding the President's

hand as he signs a government document. The cartoon was entitled 'The Two Presidents' and put the following words in Zayas's mouth: 'What happened, gentlemen? Did Crowder sign or do I?' The magazine was closed down.

ENCOURAGED BY MY GRANDMOTHER and the unexpected libertarian mayor, the small group in Lanzós evolved into a revolutionary Communist party, sending two representatives to the Socialist Congress of 1921 which produced the Socialist and Communist party split.

Ángel Castiñeira, the clandestine anarchist, and I were sent with instructions to vote for our inclusion in the Communist Party. If the truth be told, we had to swallow a lot of bile. But we respected our mandate and signed with José Lopez Darriba for Ribadeo, Eduardo Torralba for Pontevedra and Severino Chacón, of the La Coruña Tobacco Federation. Some were trade unionists, others anarchists and others socialists, but we all came home from the Congress as communists.

Out of modesty or fatigue, my grandmother did not talk much about her sentimental life during those years. But asking around in the village, I found out that her relationship with Graciano had had a profound effect, deep down. She maintained an affectionate friendship with García Kohly and Don Gabriel and they responded with proportionate largesse by keeping her and educating her son. Gossip had it that, because of a slip up by the priest – unaccustomed to these worldly necessities – she had to have more than one unsavoury abortion.

I didn't like the way they put all the blame on Gabriel. It could be that my body had been damaged by Doctor Carrión's savagery. The priest was no more nor less versed in these things than any other man. I was very fond of him, as much for his age and because his passionate nature reminded me a lot of Graciano, the man who grew on me with time and who my body will not release. Now I make love only with him. When night comes I dream he is beside me in bed, that we caress each other and end in a total embrace. It must be true because the Chinese say there is no difference between what we dream and what happened a month or week ago. I believe it is a miracle that he is alive with me. He used to say he only lived for me, and will only die when I leave this earth.

Chapter Forty-Five

DURRUTI AND ASCASO, two Spanish anarchists travelling round Spanish America, turned up in La Habana. Their aim was to kindle sympathy for their movement and, by the by, collect funds by robbing banks.

Primo de Rivera had expelled them for an attempt on the life of Alfonso XIII, which he attributed to them. After New York their final destination was to be Mexico but they came first to Cuba on forged passports. On their stopover in La Habana, I and some other anarchists went to meet them, to bring them up to date with the situation. They wanted to stay for a few days, so I accompanied them to see the Galician trade unionist Santiago Iglesias, to put the world to rights.

Iglesias had organised the famous strikes at the Compañía Arrendataria de Consumos in La Coruña. The strike leaders had to escape when the Captain General of Galicia, Sánchez Bregua, ordered troops out onto the streets. Iglesias fled to Cuba and worked in a steamship company, which enabled him to set up unions in the ports. He left the sea to work in the fruit preserves factory of *La Constancia,* and was eventually employed as a reader in *El Alemán, La Corona,* and various other sugar mills. He read to the workers from Max Stirner's *The Ego and His Own,* and Paul Lafargue's *The Right to Be Lazy,* until the owners got wind of it.

He always had time to finish reading the books because the foremen were so stupid. If they questioned him, he told them that the 'Ego' Stirner's book was referring to was God, and 'His Own' meant the people. As for Lafargue, fortunately they did not know he was born in Santiago de Cuba and was the son-in-law of Karl Marx. Iglesias explained there was a typing error in the title: it was meant to be 'crazy' not 'lazy', that Lafargue believed we all had the right to be crazy. He gradually became part of the trade union movement in Cuba and ended up as secretary of the Working Man's Club.

NOT ONLY DID SHE HAVE GRACIANO in her body, she also had him in her soul and on her conscience. She relived the conversations she had with García Kohly in which he – no doubt to hurt her when he learned the truth – told her of his arguments with the tramp who spent his days prowling round the house. Dolores went over the scene in her head: he was doing no one any harm, he obviously likes hearing the little girl play the habanera 'You', and he'll tire of it if Francisquilla doesn't change her repertory. Not for a moment did she connect the beggar with the victim of the duel; how true it is that we only understand what suits us.

The light of The Star shone for progressives and the word spread. One day Lois Peña Novo, a lawyer from Irimia, introduced himself to Miragaya. Thereafter he brought several friends, among them his brother Antonio, and Luis Pimentel, the poet from Lugo. With a copy of the Constitution and all the latest fascist decrees in his hand, Peña Novo demonstrated that there was no regulation or legal norm prohibiting the use of the Galician language in books or any other publications. He suggested they take advantage of this loophole to unite the resistance around defence of the language.

Years later, Peña Novo convinced me of the reactionaries' lack of culture and rigour by showing me some files from the Public Order Tribunal of 25th January 1938. Valle-Inclán had already lain in the Compostela cemetery for two years when this annotation was made: 'Headquarters has discovered this individual belongs to the Friends of the Soviet Union. Locate him and his records.' Days later it stated: 'Search warrant for Ramón María del Valle y Inclán sent to La Coruña, Ferrol and Santiago.' They obviously had no idea Inclán was a pseudonym, and spent several months searching in obscure corners.

And that's how magazines and books in Galician, especially poetry, came to be published, even during the war. The aforementioned Pimentel, Noriega Varel, Díaz Jácome and Anxel Fole, with Peña Novo leading them by the hand, collaborated in some of the editions. The Star gradually became a focal point for opposition to the regime of the New Spain.

AS I THINK I SAID I had been very involved with the anarchists for many years. Now Salvador Iglesias asked me to take charge of the two Spaniards whose sense of justice had led them to rebellion. They were both about twenty-eight and they spent their lives with revolution on their lips. The memory I have of Durruti is of a good, generous and sentimental man, although his main characteristic was his nobility, over and above his passion for risk. I took him to the house of Jacinto Albicoco, a man his own age, also an anarchist, but who did not share with him the strategic need to use violence. From what I could see, Albicoco was an evolutionary anarchist, if such activism exists. He received us affectionately and settled the Spaniards in his house. I accompanied them around the city, since I knew the places to avoid if we didn't want the police to see us.

Albicoco organised several meetings for the visiting anarchists. Two tendencies soon formed: one, swept along by Durruti, were ready to take direct action, while the majority, led by Iglesias and railway workers' leader Enrique Varona, thought the work of the anarchists should be educative; any other method of shortening transition to the libertarian society would be fruitless. The workers' poverty and desperation might provoke outbursts of rage, but they would go no further than that.

'Why do you think negroes don't go to your meetings?' argued Durruti. 'Because you don't invite them and you don't help them. Why do activists like yourselves, who pretend to be anarchists, live so far removed from the world of work and abandon the people in the hands of the bosses and governments you say you hate?'

'Your enterprise is headed for failure,' replied Varona. 'The Spanish and Cuban workers, despite their poverty, will donate a few pesos but nothing more. Don't expect help of any other kind. And if you start agitating, most likely you'll be deported, or be locked up in one of those Cuban prisons people only leave feet first.'

'If we want to build a movement that represents everyone,' insisted the Spaniards, 'we have to begin by questioning ourselves, and fight all forms of racism and capitalism. Propaganda is an important part of our work, of course, but theory is dead if it isn't accompanied by action, even more so given the number of illiterates the propaganda is directed at. What's more, if propaganda is not backed by a strong organisation, newspapers and journals can be shut down and the editors imprisoned.'

One of the questions the left-wing parties, liberals and anarchists, studied was the possibility of an alliance with the Communist Party which had been founded in 1925, only two months after Machado's dictatorship took power. I took the Spaniards to see Julio Antonio Mella, the student leader who had been elected to the Central Committee. Mella was categorical:

'It's time to fight, to fight with passion. Those who don't take up arms and join the struggle because of small differences of opinion are traitors or cowards. Differences can be discussed tomorrow. Today the only honourable thing to do is fight.'

Chapter Forty-Six

Dear Dolores,

Xosé is doing very well. His hostel is finished and the fibber put up a pretentious sign announcing Hotel Chao. It is already getting known around these parts. And listen to this; the relations Xosé had with the wife of a civil guard is about to make us grandmothers. Boy or girl, Xosé wants it to learn the piano, since he has a love of opera and zarzuela inherited from Cuba. I am still with Don Gabriel, our sexual encounters are no more but I still have that great affection for him which I really transferred from Graciano.

The other day I went to a funeral held in a chapel near Gondaísque. It is a place for people possessed by the devil. They are angry and often blaspheme, but after a few exorcisms and 'get thee behind me's' from the priest, they go home calmer and – not all of them, but some – even rid of the demons that inhabited them. The funeral was very strange. It reminded me of something I had seen at a Lucumbí ceremony. Six people carried the coffin, taking two steps forwards and one back in zig-zag patterns, yet when they reached the graveyard, they put it in the niche without more ado. I know that in Cuba they walk like that so the corpse is happy that his family want to keep him as long as possible. In Galicia I was told it was to disorientate the corpse so he would not return home, since the dead are much feared. The procession took place around the feast of San Juan, in the merry month of June. I suppose the little demons will have stayed in those parts, perhaps sucking on the udders of the cows and goats until autumn comes and the first signs of winter. Then, warm as toast by the fire in their rooms, they do polyglot exercises and many others that show signs of what is called madness. I am well and I pray to God, the Virgin Mary and all the saints, not forgetting Ochún and Yemayá, that I stay that way. All things considered, it would not be good if I didn't.

I miss you,
DOLORES

Chapter Forty-Seven

WHEN GENERAL MACHADO – tyrant and Liberal, President of the La Habana branch of General Electric – became President of the Republic, the Mafia and corruption took over Cuba, with men and money from Las Vegas and Chicago.

Thanks to them, Cuba had a certain air of prosperity, both in the cities and the countryside, a veneer that hid the total domination of Yankee capital. But one only had to visit the taverns and working class neighbourhoods to realise its physical and moral poverty. Prostitution was the order of the day, more so because the regime itself encouraged it.

Students and workers fought violent battles against the police and army. Julio Antonio Mella was assassinated in exile in Mexico, as was another young student, Rafael Trejo. Together with hundreds of anonymous opponents of the regime, these two deaths only served to further poison a climate of already severe unemployment and poverty.

The poet Rubén Martínez Villena managed to paralyse the country by calling a strike in March, 1930. Meanwhile, in Miami committees of refugees were created to support the struggle, and within the army itself young officers joined the opposition.

WHY SHOULD CUBA BE different from Uruguay, Chile, Argentina or Mexico, the two Spanish anarchists asked themselves? The situation on the island intrigued them, and they decided to stay for a while to see if they could help in any way.

I accompanied them to join the gangs of stevedores loading and unloading the ships in the harbour. They mixed with the workers in the taverns, and shared the hovels that served as lodging. Their workmates soon came to appreciate them; Durruti in particular, due to his corpulence

201

and propensity to always lend anyone a hand. *From their daily work they passed to confidences about the humiliations and disappointments of political parties that pitched them into action then left them in the lurch.*

Those workers had the fatalism of pariahs betrayed by their leaders but were not resigned to just slaving away and shutting up. Talking to them about organisation, however, reminded them of some leader or other who had let them down, or seeing themselves in handcuffs, being taken to a prison 'you only came out of in a box'.

'The Cuban people fought for their freedom against Spanish colonialism and won. Does falling under the domination of the dollar take away from that first victory? No, on the contrary, you need to show that fighting for political independence alone is not enough; you have to extend it to the economy. And economic independence cannot be achieved by the means the bourgeoisie propose. They tell you you're independent now, but the same ruling class maintain the same economic structures as before. Decolonisation hasn't solved any of your problems. So let's denounce false solutions by applying Bakunin's theories and at the same time show how they lead directly to human emancipation.'

Some followers of the Independent Party of Colour were won over by the anarchists, convinced that their leaders had shown themselves too accommodating to those holding power.

'That critical sense inherent in anarchism,' added Durruti and Ascaso, 'cannot be confined to gatherings of the converted. Words must be turned into actions, out in the streets and mixing with workers in the city and the countryside.'

ÁNGEL INVITED ME TO VISIT MADRID. Naturally, after having seen La Habana and New York, the only thing left for me to see was Madrid. We went in a horrible train, hours and hours in third class, carriages with wooden seats. And then, a fleapit of a hostel in Ferraz Street, but I was quite used to that lack of comfort in Cuba. The next day, Ángel confessed that we were actually going to a demonstration in La

Marañosa, a village near the capital where they made bombs of stuff called mustard gas. A Galician army corporal, also an anarchist, called Sánchez Barroso, told us that it was something like sulphur. The villagers went blind. Their skin turned black and peeled off. Cattle swelled up then died. Crops suddenly dried up. No one could drink water from the streams for weeks. The Moroccans said it was poisoned.

This mustard gas my grandmother told me about was yperite, a chemical agent which the Spanish army used in Morocco, together with phosgene, diphosgene and chloropicrin. After the massive use of chemical weapons in the First World War, the 1919 Treaty of Versailles, and the 1925 Geneva Convention decided to outlaw all manufacture, importation and use of chemical weapons. However, in contravention of international law, Spain and Germany signed an agreement in 1923 to build a chemical weapons plant in La Marañosa outside Madrid, which would be named after Alfonso XIII, in recognition of the monarch's liking for this type of weapon. The German experts concluded that mustard gas was the ideal chemical substance to bomb the Kabyles of the Rif and Yebala regions since, on top of the effect it had on the population, it permeated their fields and scarce water deposits. La Marañosa produced vast quantities of this gas for several years. Phosgene and chloropicrin bombs, dropped from aeroplanes, and land artillery were also used. The bombing campaign with toxic gases, which went on until 1927, was at its height in the period between 1924 and 1926, during Primo de Rivera's dictatorship. The strategy consisted of dropping these bombs on the most populated areas at hours when most victims could be expected. Bombing the main squares of Moroccan villages became routine.

THE CIVIL GUARD'S WIFE went to Lugo for the last months of her pregnancy, before the bulge showed, and there she gave birth to a son (the norm in her family apparently), whom Don Gabriel baptised with the names Mario Luis. The latter was the mother's choice, because it was the name of her husband (who did not know he had become a father again), and I chose Mario for García Kohly, the father of my Xosé. As your father wished, you were made to sit at the piano even as a toddler, and forced to practise scales and fingering so much, poor little thing, that at ten you gave your first recital in the Lugo Arts Club. The whole Spanish nation called you, depending on the newspaper, the Pierino Gamba, the Roberto Benzi or the Arturito Pomar of the piano.

I was your grandmother and your godmother. And despite giving you such elegant names, I always called you Chuchiño. Hearing you play was divine. We had a piano on the veranda beside my bedroom, and I never tired of listening to Schubert's 'Military March', Paderewski's 'Minuet', and especially the habanera 'You'. I always had that song on the brain, it reminded me of old times in Labana. Even more so when I learned how much it moved Graciano to listen to it. I went to La Coruña especially to buy you the partiture and after six or seven months of fierce battling, you could play it from memory perfectly.

Chapter Forty-Eight

DURRUTI AND ASCASO were also popular with the forces of repression. The police hounded them. So as not to fall into their hands, they decided to disappear from the capital, and guess what, I was designated once again to provide them with cover through the island.

The three of them left La Habana and arrived in Santa Clara. Two days later the two men were taken on as cane-cutters on a plantation between Cruces and Palmira. My grandmother pretended to be Ascaso's wife. What a life! A strike broke out two days later because under the pretext of a drop in the price of sugar, the owner reduced the cutters' wages. Encouraged by Durruti and Ascaso, they all stopped cutting. The owner gathered them together in front of the big house and reproached them for being led astray by certain well-known individuals. He chose three men at random and sent them to the local Rural Guard post. An hour later the guards reappeared with the three cane-cutters, beaten so black and blue that they fell inert at their comrades' feet.

'Any more protests? What's more, the lost time will be deducted from your wages. Back to work!'

Durruti and Ascaso returned to the canefields with the rest. Dispirited, they exchanged views with a Cuban cutter. The three agreed the owner needed to be taught a lesson.

The next morning, the owner was found dead with the words 'Rovers' justice', written on the blade of the machete. The rural guard pursued the executioners; but since we had fled at the first glimpse of dawn, by midday we were already in the province of Camagüey.

News of the execution spread like wildfire, and as it was told the dimensions grew. Word went round that a band of Spanish renegades called The Rovers had killed half a dozen plantation owners in order to take over of their property.

For the Rural Guard, hunting them down was a matter of honour. Executing The Rovers in public would be a warning to anyone thinking of following in their footsteps. In their frenzy to find us, they struck blindly out, burning huts and beating peasants accused of harbouring us. The whole thing was further complicated when it was known that a foreman had been found dead in the district of Holguín with the message from The Rovers claiming responsibility for his death. I can assure you it was not us, because we were at the other end of the island by then. But land owners and policemen alike were terrified and barricaded themselves in their territories. We escaped to Mexico.

ONE DAY CORPORAL Sánchez Barroso appeared in Lanzós. He was the one who a few months earlier had taken Ángel and I to La Marañosa to show us the mustard gas factory. He was accused of having raised the Galician, Basque and Catalan flags, together with separatists from those regions, on a boat leaving Málaga for the war in Morocco. A non-commissioned officer from the Royal Engineers was killed when he tried to overpower the separatists. Barroso was held responsible and condemned to death. He escaped and took refuge with us. We hid him in the attic of the Cultural Club.

Barroso was a soldier of conservative ideas, who could have avoided military service because he was a widow's son, but he preferred to 'defend his country'. After a year in the barracks, he realised the true significance of the Africa campaign and contacted movements that opposed it. Various figures on the right intervened and asked for his sentence to be commuted to a lesser charge. Among his champions were the Cardinal Primate and Prince Carlos, Captain General of Seville, who had originally confirmed the sentence of the court in Málaga. In Barcelona, radical members of parliament and councillors petitioned for the same cause and asked the civil governor, Señor Portela, to transmit the request to Madrid.

THE SÁNCHEZ BARROSO CASE *caused a public outcry. Ángel went to Madrid to drum up support from friends while the corporal stayed in Lanzós, scared to death. General Bermúdez de Castro, Minister of War, decreed the Barroso judgement be annulled, given that Prince Carlos had not wanted to sign the sentence. It was invalidated, but after a new trial, with the same sentence, the soldier faked an accident, so the final decision was postponed again. In Galicia, we organised protests against the sentence, particularly in La Coruña, where we succeeded in getting all shops to close. Our friend was finally pardoned.*

THE DUSTY STREETS OF MEXICO CITY, dirty and dilapidated, still betrayed traces of the Revolution. The machine guns of the 'bloody decade' had left their mark on the walls. At ten at night there was not a soul in the streets, and the anarchists spent the night talking to Diego Rivera.

They did the talking, alone with him, since I was a woman and not really convinced by anarchism, and they were bound to have a lot to discuss. Finally, late and tired, Diego Rivera went back to his painting. I was left to snoop around his house.

I never saw anyone so attached to his country. Everything in his house was Mexican: rugs, furniture made and painted by Indians, tri-coloured doors from Oaxaca. In the corridors were pieces of pottery, a marvellous selection of handcrafted jars, plates, and flagons. The rooms were full of deities from different periods of Aztec culture. And on the walls, a plethora of paintings 'that now I think are bad' he said, even though he had painted them the night before. I remember two or three very sombre works of Indian women, sitting just as I had seen them on the train that brought us from Vera Cruz to Mexico City.

It was an old colonial house with wooden staircases and iron-studded doors. In it lived and worked this ugly giant, a force of nature open to all the most generous ideas, who didn't believe in art for art's sake, but in a living art, art to be lived. He told us he was ruminating on the composition of a fresco for the Simón Bolívar amphitheatre of the National Preparatory School. When Rivera went up to his workshop, the scaffolding creaked under the weight of his body. He always had two bricklayers with him preparing the surfaces so he could paint them while they were still wet. Every now and then, he would skip down a ladder, with astounding agility, and bite on a green chilli as he surveyed the effect of the colour.

Durruti was captivated by Rivera because he always wore a revolver at his waist. I suppose he dreamed of having him in The Rovers.

'It's to guide the critics,' said Rivera, stopping Durruti short just in case.

ÁNGEL CASTIÑEIRA'S LIBERTARIAN IDEAS were becoming increasingly clear. He wanted to fight, he wanted the government to arm the people and stop doing shady deals with the Fascists: like Casares Quiroga who had just suggested giving a ministry to General Mola. He formed a resistance committee made up, among others, of Lois Peña Novo, Miragaya, the school teacher, the vet, and my grandmother. It prepared to confiscate weapons from the police; detain right-wing elements – the priest among them – and keep them in secret hide-outs as a precaution; watch the roads into town and other strategic places; and ostracise various municipal officials, especially the Falangist Antonio Boado Pernas.

THE CUBAN AUTHORITIES WERE NOT UNAWARE of Dolores's work with the revolutionary press. They also knew she was an audacious activist. No sooner had she got off the boat than two armed policemen detained her on the quayside. 'Follow us,' they said without even asking who she was. They took her to the sector of the Morro prison called 'The Boarding School'.

We disembarked in the late afternoon, and reached the prison as night fell. The cell already had four inmates. I was lucky to get myself a piece of floor space just large enough to doss down on. The straw mattresses showed signs of having serviced hundreds of prisoners, but nevertheless crackled when I lay down. I needed a cover for the night. I had been given an old army blanket but it wasn't enough. Fortunately one of the prisoners gave me a shawl that must have been of good quality in its day. The others were angry at the noise I was making. The next day, they kept harassing me and asking if I were a thief, a prostitute or the author of some bloody crime. 'No, I'm a communist.' 'Really? Can women be communists too? Teach us, then,' said my protector.

That same night, after the guards had done their last check, the women's block became a conference hall. I told them what made women turn to crime and prostitution; what communism meant for us women; about the Soviet Union and the situation of women in socialist countries, comparing it to the life they led in Cuba.

It was not long before the nun in charge of our block came to see me. With the most hypocritical of smiles, she told me the mother superior had decided to transfer me to a small attic where the kitchen staff slept. Our block was insalubrious and I would find the other room more comfortable. Although I benefitted, and was happy to change, I realised only too well that they were trying to prevent all subversive talk.

My stay in prison was disagreeable, especially because of certain personal anxiety. A few days after my detention, a guard told me a young man of about fifteen who said he was my Xosé was at the prison gates. They were going to send him to the swamps to fight what was left of the Independents of Colour, and they were going to make sure he was on the most dangerous front line. I knew it was impossible, because Xosé was being well looked after by some relatives of Monguita in a black neighbourhood, where the police dared not go.

The fact made Dolores reflect on many things. One of them she left in writing:

'Life proved yet again how hard it is for a wife and mother to devote herself to the revolutionary struggle. Life, liberty, none of it matters… but our children! Do we have the right to sacrifice them, and deprive them, by our own hazardous existence, of a mother's care, attention, and love? This was always one of the most painful aspects of my life, although I didn't talk about it much, because I had always thought that the best way of teaching and persuading was to lead by example, however many tears of blood it cost.'

THE FIRST OF MAY APPROACHED and she was going to have to spend it in prison. During meetings in which she told her prison companions of the demonstrations and deaths in Chicago, Dolores explained the significance of that day and taught them a verse of 'The Internationale'.

The moment arrived. The long-serving inmates had in their memories the songs the nuns had taught them: the Salve Regina *and submissive Christian hymns. That 1st May the repertory was to undergo certain changes. After breakfast, they formed up in the patio and began to sing:*

Arise, ye workers from your slumbers
Arise, ye prisoners of want
For reason in revolt now thunders
And at last end the age of cant

Shortly before ten at night it was grub time. We went out into the deserted alley, and there, in Indian file, we marched one behind the other to an enormous stockpot where with a spoon, which also served as a measure, they gave us a most ghastly soup of lentils and noodles. Although I had no appetite, I tried the broth, but as I put the spoon in that dented aluminium plate, I shuddered at the rasping of the spoon with the bottom of the bowl; but I was far more scandalised by the crunch of an earthy substance that grated against my teeth.

A young friendly schoolteacher named Pilar explained it was because stones were put in the bags of dry vegetables so that they weigh more, and the rubbish was all dumped in the stockpot and cooked without being washed or sorted. You can understand, she added in a playful tone, that for those at the top to be fat, those at the bottom have to get a goodly ration of watery gruel, a lot of scraps and a few, a very few lentils.

'THOSE WHO SING 'THE INTERNATIONALE', that separatist riffraff paid by Russia, who aim to confuse the people and deprive them of their traditional core values of religion and culture, are trying to destroy us. The Moscow International, under whose Asiatic tyranny we found ourselves, is now loosening its tragic grip on our motherland. The second Spanish War of Independence is ending, like the first in 1808. Our side, which this present government of Jews and Free Masons calls seditious, guarantees your right to work. The other side, which upsets the work process with strikes and lockouts, will be shot without trial.'

They listened to the radio dispatches in the Social Club; it was always the same, the Nationalists had taken this town or that town; the Reds had had to surrender this place or that place. Enrique Marínas commented on the glorious actions of the Galicians forcibly recruited onto the Aragón front:

'Their spirit is such that on leaving their frozen white trenches, bravely over-running enemy positions after their victorious battles, they took out the bagpipes they had carried tenaciously over the cold lands of *la jota*, and played a *muñeira* as an anthem to the Caudillo of Ferrol, General Franco.'

A PEEPHOLE OPENED and someone yelled at them to shut up. The group carried on singing, with Dolores conducting. Eventually the loud-mouthed director of the Morro prison arrived. 'That is not allowed in an official establishment. No one goes hungry here and women are not oppressed. If you want to enjoy yourselves, sing the Gregorian chant "Pange Lingua".' Meanwhile the prisoners kept on singing. Dolores turned her head to inform him he hadn't forbidden the singing of religious hymns the previous day, which he should have done so according to the democratic rule of three, and then turned back to the singing angels to urge them to put more energy into the song.

The director swept off slamming the door and that night took his miserable revenge by giving us some inedible grub. I organised such a ruckus that they turned on all the prison lights. Passers-by stopped to listen, officers ran up and down the stairs, and finally an electric dialogue with the director:

'You have brought indiscipline, disorder, and rebellion, to this reformatory. I am going to tame you with all the means at my disposal.'

'I will request a parliamentary commission, señor director. For better or worse, we live in a Republic. I don't think you'll come out of an inspection with flying colours.'

Elfidio, that was the director's name, tried one more dirty trick. He offered to help some veteran prisoners with their cases if they gave me a good hiding. It was a euphemism: we all remembered how frequent prison murders were, like that of José Cuixart in La Cabaña. The attempt failed, because the others protected me. Señor Elfidio had no alternative but to swallow his pride and soften the prison regime.

Six months later, Dolores was released with no charges pending, but from then on the police had her on file as a front line political activist. Her face began to be known and sought by the regime's thugs. She would have to go into hiding or return to Spain.

EXECUTIONS WERE RARELY individual. They were held in the early mornings and *en masse*. The Reds were taken to Abadín and used ammunition to maximum effect with just one firing squad.

As dawn broke, shouts of 'Long live the Republic! Long live Democracy! Long live Socialism!' could be heard, and almost simultaneously a volley of rifle fire.

In the lorry, despite there being more than five men, you could hear a pin drop. They were paralysed; their blood congealed just like pigs, begging your pardon, when one is killed in front of the others.

In fact, they kept silent so they could count the coups de grâce *fired by the platoon officer. One shot for each body, except in special cases when, to be absolutely sure, two or three bullets were squandered on the same person.*

When those moments passed, life, gradually, began again, and a new day dawned. Some fled to the mountains, others went to eternity, and the world kept on turning.

DEAR DOLORES,

Don't be surprised if we haven't seen each other in all this time. It is seventeen years since I left Galicia, my native land; as it is yours, of course. I have travelled the countryside in La Habana, Matanzas, Camagüey, and visited some of the most beautiful cities on earth, La Coruña, Mexico and New York. But as is natural in human beings, no matter how far they are from their homeland, they never stop loving it. I felt nostalgia and a burning desire to return and settle in our country; so strong was it that I won't waste another minute preparing my things for the journey home. What pains me most, and breaks my heart, is learning of the death of my mother, whom I always loved, as you know. I want you to know also that Mario is very good to me and Xosé. He gives me money for his studies and clothes. Apparently they are going to appoint him ambassador to Madrid, so he will be nearer at hand for us. No sooner did I see the boy in the portrait you sent me, among the other children, that I guessed it was our Arturo, God rest his soul, for his likeness to him. I can't tell you how sad I was to know he passed into God's mercy. But, praise be to him in the Highest, my pain was helped by the consolation of being able to see the features of our brother reproduced in our sons.

WE HAD PLANNED A MEETING *at which La Pasionaria would speak about the situation of women, and Santiago Álvarez on the strategy of the Communist Party. We had to cancel it. A rumour spread round the village that Gumersindo Longueiras, who was married to the schoolteacher at San Simón de la Cuesta, had gone to the mountains. We had to do something urgent to help him. Gumersindo was known to be one of the most heretical freethinkers in the region. His brother-in-law Don Francisco, a canon, had a promising career in the church hierarchy. At the very least, he would be named Bishop of Mondoñedo. Gumersindo was one of the first to learn of the Fascist coup, and fast on its heels came threats on his life.*

One night he came to Lanzós and sought refuge in my house. This was like the lamb entering the lion's den, for the reputation I had. I hid him in the false ceiling in the loft where we kept the maize, the potatoes and salt pork. It would not be easy for them to find him. He only left his cubby hole at two or three in the morning to stretch his legs in the vegetable patch. I advised him to lie flat on his face and make the sign of the cross whenever anyone passed, which is the way we scare off ghosts, and crawl home without being seen. He stayed there terrified during the time it took me to go to the seminary in Mondoñedo and talk to Don Francisco. When the priest saw me, knowing who I was, he refused to listen. He had repeatedly told his brother-in-law not to get involved in politics, and now all I could do was pray for him.

'I'll be praying for his soul, Don Francisco, if we don't do something, and quickly.'

'May the will of God be done, Señora Dolores.'

The following day, the civil guard came to my house. They turned it upside down and found him curled up in the hidey-hole. They took him away, beating him as they went. Lois Peña Novo offered to defend him.

Such resistance would not go unpunished. One September afternoon my grandmother was sitting at the door of The Star Cultural Club waiting for her comrades. Three months after Franco's uprising, in Lanzós we still knew little of what was happening in the rest of Spain; the radio only broadcast triumphant dispatches about the advance of the rebel soldiers, and the imminent extermination of the Communist and Masonic rabble; and the newspapers were rigidly censured. News of the execution of army officers loyal to the Republic, like Pita da Veiga in La Coruña, only reached us clandestinely by word of mouth, and rumours abounded that this doctor, or that progressive mayor, had been dumped in a ditch with a bullet in the neck.

I saw a large cloud of dust in the distance, followed by the drone of a car engine. Instinct told me to bury a trunk full of the committee's documents in the garden. The noise grew louder and a truckload of beardless babes in gaiters, navy blue shirts, with pistols at their waists, burst into the yard.

They were very rude. When I asked in whose name they were disturbing the town's peace, one said:

'Señora, I don't have to explain anything to you, but if you're interested, it is in the name of Spaaaaiiiin!'

Without further impertinence, they went into The Star and began destroying everything they could lay hands on – the typewriter and an ancient daguerreotype – we didn't have much else. Outside the club they made a pile of desks, books, Galician and Republican flags, a portrait of Rosalía, and then set fire to it.

One of the babes took a proclamation out of his pocket and, having rounded up the inhabitants of the village, read it out in the light of the bonfire:

'Young men of Galicia! The Falange is assembling a powerful column to fight for God and Spaaaiiiin. A quarter of our nation's territory is still in the hands of the Reds and it is of the utmost urgency that we rescue it for Spaaaiiiin.

'Galician! If you want others to believe in the bravery and daring you pride yourself in, and that your brothers have displayed with their heroic deeds on the battle fronts; if you are a proud and honourable man; if you love the Motherlaaaaaand: Enlist voluntarily here, at this recruiting office of the Spanish Falange! Long live Spaaaiiiin!'

Then, with a large bucket of paste, they proceeded to daub the town with posters in the form of edicts. By order of the civil governor, it set out the six planks of the new Catholic-Francoist morality:

1. Dress modestly: no exaggerated necklines, skirts and sleeves.
2. Do not go out without stockings. Wear mended stockings rather than none at all. If money is the problem, eliminate bars and cinemas.
3. Reduce make-up on the face and lips. Do not use inappropriate hair colour. Certain girls forsake their

natural beauty and paint themselves like shop window mannequins.

4. Women alone or even couples are not to behave in inappropriate ways, especially frequenting isolated dimly-lit places.

5. Women are forbidden to smoke: it is a very unladylike habit. If a woman wants to smoke, let her take up a rifle, put on an overall, and leave for the front.

6. Devote as much time as possible to looking after our troops and the wounded, and reduce your number of outings and unnecessary spending.

These six points will come into effect as soon as they are published. The public will see to it that they are carried out, without the intervention of the authorities; it would be a pity if we did have to intervene but we would certainly do so if these points are not respected because we live in a time of blind obedience and respect for our mandate.'

The Falange installed a desk in the self same recently pillaged Cultural Club, at which they proceeded to make a list of the donations the inhabitants were coerced into offering:

Little Xulio Andrade Lemos: a goat.

Señora Josefa, admirer of the glorious army: a *salchicha* and a dozen *chorizos*.

Señor Bouzas: four chickens and four pieces of salt cod.

Ester Ramudo Otero: a box of quince jelly.

África Souto Varela: three rabbits.

A lady who wants peace: four tins of oil, a total of forty litres.

Camila Álvarez Graña: four sacks of potatoes.

Doña Eudosia Ponte Cascudo: a ham.

The servant of the aforementioned: three kilos of rice.

A patriot: a box of sweets.

An admirer of the Infantry: two pigs and a sheep.

The following day, there was not a young lad or animal to be seen around these parts. Some of them took to the mountains, others emigrated. Three days later, the morons were back. They were looking for Miragaya.

'THEY'RE GOING TO SHOOT ME. I've no way out.'

'Don't say that. Peña Novo will make a case for you.'

'It's not that I don't think he's capable of it. If there is a moral case he'll find it, but not with these people, they answer only to their God and country. The only thing awaiting me is a passport to the other world.'

He stood there, head bowed, for a few moments.

'Not only did I not join the uprising, I was also caretaker of The Star. The other day they profaned it by hanging a Birth of Jesus with Three Kings on the wall. I couldn't bear it. I came in with a club, and started swinging left, right and centre: the donkeys went flying; the baby Jesus drowned in the stream; and Melchior, Caspar and Balthasar lost their crowns, their clothes hung in tatters like beggars. I signed my death warrant there and then.'

They caught Miragaya and finished him off in Vilarrube. In his pocket, they found a letter from his grandson written by the authorities, since Gabrieliño could have been no more than six.

> *Dear Three Kings,*
>
> *I hope you'll remember me this year and give me a little present, for which I will be very grateful. I promise to be good, always be a loyal servant, obey Spain and our Caudillo, to whom I owe this great joy. I put all my hope in Him, in God and in you,*
>
> *Respectfully, Gabriel*

Miragaya's death certificate says:

> By the order of the judge, I deliver to you the present
> in order that you may proceed to inscribe in the Civil
> Register the death of Eugenio Paradela Baliño, 65
> years old, married, son of Germán and Pilar, domiciled
> in Lanzós, for want of any other information, whose
> dead body was found on the side of the main road near
> Vilarrube, parish of Irimia, last 14th August, and died
> of an internal haemorrhage, having been buried in the
> cemetery of the said parish of Irimia on the 15th of
> the said month.
> Irimia, 4th November 1936

WE HAVE TO ADMIT THAT, apart from cursory executions, they did pass lesser sentences that were less than death and thirty years in jail. But there were not very many of them, because setting up the whole machinery of war tribunals just to hand out small punishment would be pointless. The precursors of what years later came to be called 'productivity' had to give the example of optimum performance so the percentage of death sentences had to be high. Those who had the good luck not to win in this death lottery deserved more congratulations than if they had won the jackpot. They held Peña Novo's trial in Lugo and condemned him to death:

'Very dangerous individual: notorious extremist; a member of The Star Cultural Club in the village of Lanzós; and previous to that one of the founders of the Brotherhood of the Language. Together with Castelao, he wrote the so-called *Statute of Galicia*, and ended up in the ORGA with Casares Quiroga, whom he tried to orientate towards Galician identity and the political left. As a member of the workers and peasants' block, he helped organise the POUM, and was its leader while the Reds controlled Llanes. With a record of activism in the revolutionary events of 1934, he spoke at the meeting in the main square of Quintana besides abominable figures like Castelao, Alejandro Bóveda, and Antón Villar Ponte. He was the civil governor of Valencia under the Red domination and helped organise the first antifascist war committee in the town. He was, in the opinion of various witnesses, the most influential member of that committee, and to all intents and purposes gave the orders in the town. The Reds had so much confidence in him that they appointed him Governor General of Extremadura, where he introduced agrarian reform. The town council in which he played such a prominent role was responsible for numerous outrages, like arbitrary imposition of fines, destruction of religious objects, weapons collection, registration and detention of a large number of people, among them four inhabitants of the town. The accused intervened personally in the detention of these patriots and, according to several witnesses, even went so far as to apprehend them himself. The victims of this crime were a gentleman by the name of Couceiro, a brother of the village priest, and two other priests in the vicinity.'

They allowed him to make a statement. Peña Novo rose to his feet and said:

> Do not think, señor, that either you or the head of investigation of the organism which you preside, that this crime will go unpunished, because do not forget I leave two children and a wife, who in due time will demand justice. All the evidence you now provide may one day need to be justified in front of a judge. But do not try to hide your responsibility, since all our comrades who have been in prison, all those who are in exile, my relatives and the whole Spanish people know, without any shadow of doubt, that you are condemning an innocent man.

FOR HIS COMPLICITY WITH US and out of envy for the
resplendent life he lead, Don Gabriel was sent to end his days in the
Franciscan convent of Los Picos, near Mondoñedo, by the new bishop, the
very harsh pro-Franco Benjamín de Arriba y Castro. Because of my age,
because I was a woman, and I think because García Kohly intervened, I
was put under house arrest, in perpetuity. My son Xosé was denounced as
a Red by the cuckolded civil guard, and was also put under house arrest
with me. I was supposed to report to the civil guard headquarters in Irimia
every day. But in small towns arrangements are made. My son installed
me in this room in the hostel he had just inaugurated, and went to the
civil guard barracks to sign for the two of us.

THE GLORIOUS STAR CULTURAL CLUB, which had gone
through so much, ended up with a new sign: 'Eternal Spain'. The
fascists converted it into a sewing workshop for making uniforms
for the front, after requisitioning all women with a minimum
knowledge of the art of needlework. The poor nuns went back
to their life of seclusion in the convent. A call to action by the
authorities dominated the place:

> 'Galician woman: Nothing can be more relevant than
> Quevedo's phrase: "Women are instruments for losing
> kingdoms". It encapsulates the power of your influence
> over the world. One of the most important battles in
> history is being waged in our beloved Homeland, and
> in it you have the place of honour. All men worthy
> of our honourable and powerful Homeland are at the
> front fighting for the Caudillo to liberate Spain from
> the Red tyranny. They have modern weapons and their
> spirits are high, but they also need a sanctuary, and it is
> up to you to provide it for them.
>
> 'The organisation Mothers in the Service of Spain,
> in whose ranks over 4,000 good patriots serve, have
> already made about 35,000 uniforms and we need to

increase production. Not a single woman must fail to answer the call.

'Long live Spain! Long live Generalissimo Franco!'

I WAS GIVEN THE DEATH SENTENCE TOO, but in Irimia arrangements could always be made. Your father had a hotel-restaurant, and food was beginning to be short. By using chorizos and hams, he managed to get the death penalty commuted to house arrest. He put on several banquets for the authorities for which he did not charge, so they allowed him to sign for me at the civil guard barracks when he signed for himself. I have the pardon document in that drawer.

LA CORUÑA 13th DECEMBER 1936 – The Minister of War of the Spanish state having declared that the death penalty imposed on Dolores González Verdes in this case be commuted to the one immediately below; be advised that reclusion in perpetuity be imposed on the above-mentioned Dolores González Verdes and pass the notification and implementation files of this sentence to the Examining Magistrate. Commander-in-Chief of Division... (Illegible signature. Ink stamp saying: Chief of Staff Eighth Division).

On the petition of the person concerned, and as an extension of the previous testimony, I authorise this in Vigo on the thirtieth of July one thousand nine hundred thirty seven.

Examining magistrate for Vigo, Alfonso Fidalgo Pereira, Second Lieutenant of the Army Legal Corps – signed –.

Sister Maria J. Uribesalgo, Mother Superior of the Sisters of Mercy and Charity, charged with the internal running of the same.

I certify that this is a faithful copy of the original which is in the possession of inmate of this prison Dolores González Verdes.

And so all the previous can take effect, I issue this certificate in Saturrarán on the fourteenth of December one thousand nine hundred and forty two.

Mother Superior (RTD)
Sister Maria J. Uribesalgo

Still reading, I looked at the woman in front of me. I could not see her eyes. I thought of the harsh times she lived through. Her face looked drained of blood and her hands were withered; withered and furrowed with wrinkles. I held them in mine.

You have inherited my memories now, Chuchiño, take care not to make me look bad in what you write in my name.

'Your story, Grandma, is truly extraordinary. You know that by entrusting to me your memory, the epic novel of your life, the goddesses are sparing you any further trouble, because I'll try my utmost to make the narrative reflect your wishes.'

Come, Chuchiño, play 'You' for me…

I was almost twenty and she still called me Chuchiño.

I played the habanera with my heart and soul and considerable apprehension, because in Galicia we are very afraid of the dead. I felt she was about to leave me for the other world and here I was playing her a kind of *danzón*, whose languid syncopated rhythm was really upsetting me.

SHE HAD NEVER BEEN IN VIGO BEFORE. No one was expecting her. She went to the Hostal Berbés and calculated from memory how long the money Don Mario had given her would last: the mail-coach from Vigo to Compostela, five pesetas; the night in Compostela, two; another five from Compostela to Lugo; two *reales* from Lugo to Irimia, from there to Lanzós seven kilometres on foot, free as usual. She had five *reales* left for breakfast, lunch and dinner. If she did not fritter it, she could even buy a little present for Dolores.

I FINISHED PLAYING. I went back to her side and stroked her cold forehead. We still had time to exchange a few words. She kept pressing my hands until hers gradually faltered and I could slide mine out.

Ramón Chao (Villalba, Lugo 1935) is a distinguished writer and journalist. He was chief editor for the Latin American service of Radio France Internationale, and worked for *Le Monde* and *Le Monde Diplomatique*. He is the French correspondent for Radio Colifata in Buenos Aires. In 1984 he created the prestigious Juan Rulfo Prize, an award for new Spanish language writers. He has written numerous essays and novels in French, Spanish and Galician. Amongst his works are *The Train of Ice and Fire, Las Travesías de Luis Gontán, Las Andaduras del Che* and *El Lago de Como*. He lives in Paris.

Ann Wright has translated seventeen books from Spanish and French including *Motorcycle Diaries, The Train of Ice and Fire, Away From the Light of Day* and *I, Rigoberta Menchu*. She is a human rights activist and lectures on the theory and practice of civilian protection. She lives in London.

For more information on this book
and for Route's full list of titles please visit
www.route-online.com